Scorpions' Ascent

SCORPIONS ASCENT

A NOVEL

HOLLISA ALEWINE

NEW YORK

LONDON • NASHVILLE • MELBOURNE • VANCOUVER

SCORPIONS ASCENT

A Novel

Published in New York, New York, by Morgan James Publishing. Morgan James is a trademark of Morgan James, LLC. www.MorganJamesPublishing.com

Scripture references are from the NASB unless otherwise noted.

Proudly distributed by Publishers Group West®

A **FREE** ebook edition is available for you or a friend with the purchase of this print book.

_____

CLEARLY SIGN YOUR NAME ABOVE

Instructions to claim your free ebook edition:
1. Visit MorganJamesBOGO.com
2. Sign your name CLEARLY in the space above
3. Complete the form and submit a photo of this entire page
4. You or your friend can download the ebook to your preferred device

ISBN 9781636986012 paperback
ISBN 9781636986029 ebook
Library of Congress Control Number:
2024948748

Cover Design by:
Alejandra Urquide

Interior Design by:
Chris Treccani
www.3dogcreative.net

Morgan James is a proud partner of Habitat for Humanity Peninsula and Greater Williamsburg. Partners in building since 2006.

Get involved today! Visit: www.morgan-james-publishing.com/giving-back

For Nahmer. My guide, my guard, my friend for a brief moment. I'll meet you on Givat Chatzeva. We loved you.

Acknowledgments

Many thanks to Blossoming Rose, beginning with Dr. DeWayne Coxon and Lexie, Rob and Jodi, the Board, and the decades of visiting volunteers for their unrelenting devotion to preserving the history of Tamar. Without your effort, I would not have the opportunity for so many learning days and the quiet time to hear. Nahmer is buried there in an unmarked grave, but many nights I would wake in my caravan to the sound of him barking and chasing away unwelcome predators. He made sure every visitor made it safely back from a hike up the givah, and he listened to many a wise and foolish discussion in the sukkah at night.

For those interested in expert academic research and archaeology of the area, the published papers of Tali Erickson-Gini are a gold mine of information.

Thanks to Audrey M., Carol W., Jerry B., Tim and Tammy H., Teresa C, Michelle S. and family, and Doug and Dee J. for critiquing the manuscript. As someone who's walked the grounds of Tamar, Scorpions' Ascent, and the Arava, Audrey's input was invaluable. Rebecca Dowty has been an excellent developmental editor and visionary.

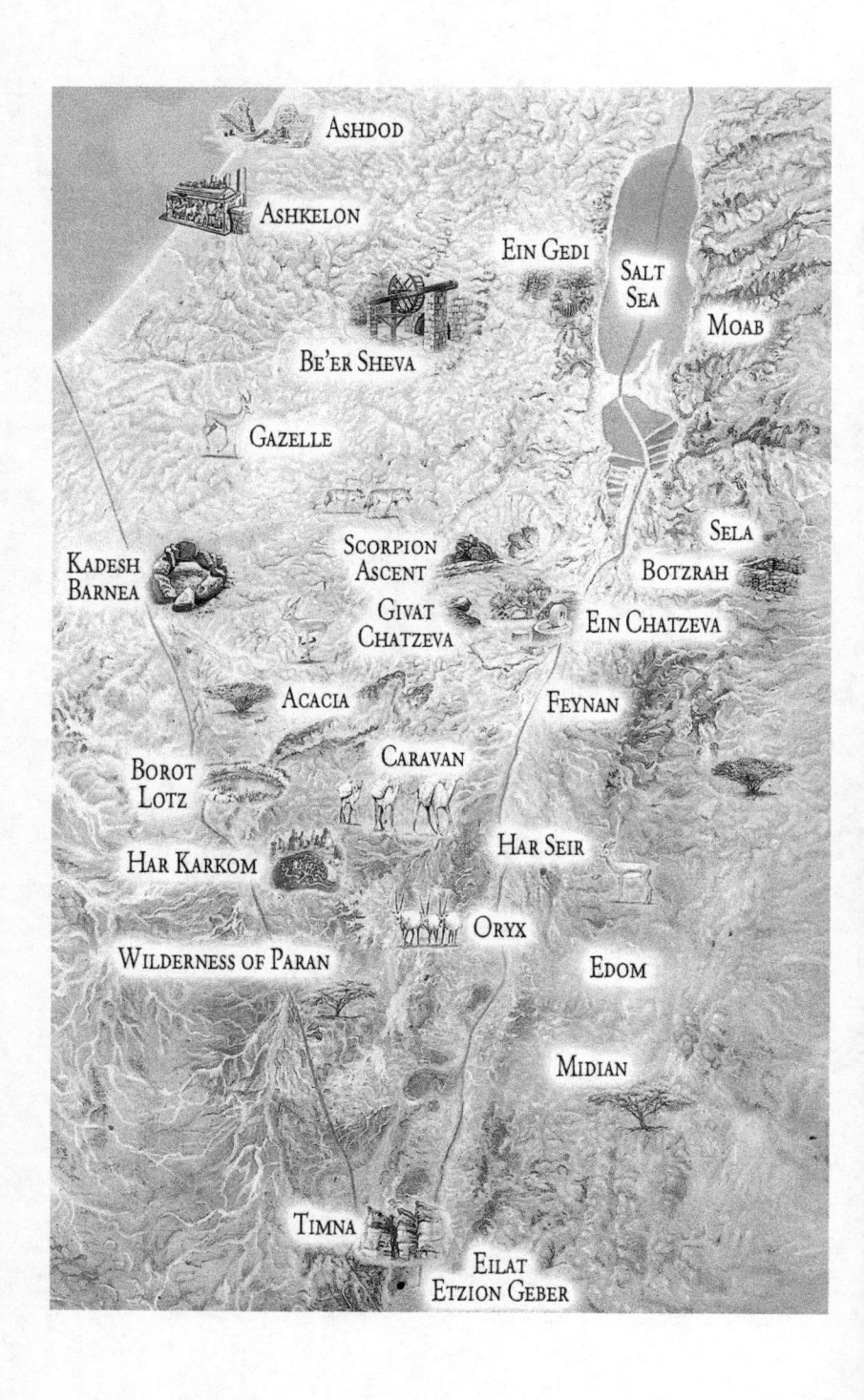

CHAPTER ONE

The camels groaned, yawned, belched, and farted to the tinkle of bells, drovers' shouts, and the creaking of their heavy baggage. Only their hooves in the sand were silent. The sun's orange glow rose in the east, prepared to slip warm fingers atop the mountains of Moab and vault into the desert sky. By noon, the sun's morning kiss would become a demonic *sheid*[1] erasing every cool shadow of the caravansary.[2]

The silver-haired boy slipped the few coins he'd earned into the leather pouch around his neck and concealed it beneath his tunic. Never let anyone see a money purse, even if your father is the steward over the king's copper mines...even if your father has a detachment of soldiers and a fortress.

Tzakhi[3] had been saving coins and product samples from the caravan merchants for several years. In return for helping them load their camels and donkeys, carrying baggage, or handing girth straps to them from beneath the soft bellies of the animals in the pre-dawn darkness, they paid him with trinkets, beads, coins, and samples of spices.

---

1   demon
2   A way station for traveling caravans where they can rest, buy food, and trade for new pack animals.
3   In Hebrew, "scorching, to be dazzling white"

The drovers and merchants who needed to trade weary or lame animals remembered him. They knew that he'd helpfully point out the strongest camels and donkeys in the nearby stone holding pens of rested stock for sale or trade. They always paid something. Tzakhi started helping the caravan merchants when he was six years old. Now that he was twelve, he'd saved jars full of coin and acquired clay juglets full of various spices. His favorites were cinnamon and saffron.

The angry shout of a caravan drover disrupted Tzakhi's thoughts. Tzakhi adjusted his turban to conceal the silver strands of hair. His *pe-ot*[4] often worked their way out of the cloth because they were so long. He scanned the last of the caravan's sluggish marchers for the source of the shouting.

The camels and donkeys were conditioned by hundreds of miles of desert sand, rocky mountains, and relentless sun to expect nothing greater than a little fodder and the shedding of their heavy burdens when the sun set. Some of the caravansary drovers were kind, some not. All were strictly business. One of them was angry.

The drover cursed again in the morning twilight. He kicked a fallen donkey, then kicked at her foal, who didn't dodge the first kick, but smartly stayed out of sandal range after that.

The nursing mother didn't even try to dodge the blows. She simply lay beneath her pack, head down, muzzle to the sand, too weak or hopeless to flinch. Her foal was only a couple of weeks old, probably nursing vainly because her dam was skinny and sick. The ailing donkey could no longer carry a burden.

"Bilaam," muttered Tzakhi, approaching the enraged drover.

"What?" asked the drover, whirling to face him.

---

4   Untrimmed sideburns worn by Jewish males; Leviticus 19:27

Tzakhi didn't repeat what he called him. It was worse than a curse word to an Israelite, but the nations around Israel knew who Bilaam was. A legendary donkey-beating sorcerer.

Ben-Shimi, the soldier of the gate that morning, looked on in the gloom, but he didn't try to help. He was supposed to check all who passed through Tamar to see if they were spies looking for weaknesses in the fortress. Supposed to. Right now, he simply leaned on his spear unsympathetically.

"I will unpack her for you so she can stand," said Tzakhi.

"Quit trying to work me for coins, boy," growled the drover.

"I want nothing," said Tzakhi. "But the front of your caravan is already past Givat Chatzeva. You'll never catch them if she can't rise. Not today, anyway."

The man's camels were already loaded, standing ready. Tzakhi let him feel the pressure of being left behind. Pressure was the best bargaining tool Tzakhi had at his age. People would pay for his help if it secured a safer position in the caravan. Bandits preyed on those who lagged.

"She'll never stand up," said the drover. "She was sick before she even foaled this miserable little camel-flea."

"Then shall I move her burden to one of the camels?" asked Tzakhi. "Before your caravan crosses the steps of the Scorpions' Ascent without you? The mountains will close you in there. It is not good to be alone."

"Yes, you little robber," fumed the drover. "I know how you caravansary boys work. You say you charge nothing, and then after you do it, you ask for payment."

Rather than answer, Tzakhi used skilled fingers to search out the knots until he lifted the burden from the fallen donkey. When he lifted, he understood why she'd fallen. The pack was too heavy for a healthy donkey, but for a sick donkey with a nursing foal?

This was pure cruelty. The man could not be a drover. Drovers knew their animals' limits. This man was a merchant.

The merchant growled and smacked one of his camels with his staff until the camel grunted and bawled and folded his knees to accept the extra baggage. Tzakhi added the burden to the kneeling camel, positioning it where it could be most easily carried. "Hurry," urged the merchant, hovering over Tzakhi. Tzakhi could tell from the camel's pack that he was a better packer than the merchant, but still he kept silent, deftly fastening the ropes.

"How much do you want?" asked the merchant when he finished.

"Nothing," answered Tzakhi, choking back the price he really wanted. He'd learned from Edomite and Nabatean traders how to bargain. "You better hurry. There is a place in the road where a winter flood washed it out. You need to catch your caravan so you'll know where to have your camels go around it." Pressure.

"Will you take the donkeys?" asked the merchant.

That was no payment. A dying donkey whose carcass would have to be removed with her foal, who would die without her milk. The merchant was offering Tzakhi nothing but more work, a sad walk to the death wadi.[5] Tzakhi folded his arms and frowned, swinging his gaze from the donkey to her foal, then looking over his shoulder to the smelting furnace atop Givat Chatzeva. He shook his head.

"I'd have to drag them a long way to the boneyard," countered Tzakhi. "The captain will not allow animal corpses around the fortress. There are wolves and jackals in the wadi who feed on the dead animals. He doesn't want them here around the tents and livestock. I have to go now to deliver food to the workers at the Chatzeva furnace."

---

5   A streambed that is usually dry except during the rainy season.

There was a wadi along the way to the Scorpions' Ascent where sick animals were disposed of. Sometimes they were simply stripped of their halters and burdens and turned loose in the desert. Sometimes the drover mercifully cut their throats so they would die within a few seconds. It was kinder than being torn to death by hyenas or jackals, which was both a terror and a painful way to die.

"Israelite robbers," muttered the merchant. Ben-Shimi stood a little straighter at the insult, finally moving.

The accusation rattled loose the words of a song in Tzakhi's memory. *"So long ago, so long ago,"* sang Tzakhi's mother in Hebrew as he fell asleep.

There was a man of the earth, a man of the sea.
His father was taken by robbers, killed by robbers.
The man went into the forest, went into the wolves.
So long ago, so long ago.

Pulling a leather pouch from inside his tunic and tugging the drawstring, the donkey-beater explored in the purse with a forefinger. "The donkeys and a bit of balsam." He extended his hand, and a tiny pearl of balsam lay in his palm.

Tzakhi hesitated, drawing out the seconds of being left behind, letting the urgency simmer. *"Two* dead donkeys," Tzakhi reminded him.

"Two pearls of balsam," offered the agitated man, sorting another nugget of resin from the pouch.

Tzakhi inclined his head. *"Sagur."*[6]

---

6   It's a deal.

CHAPTER TWO

Ben-Shimi smirked at him and rubbed his spear between his palms idly. "At least you'll smell better than two dead donkeys."

Tzakhi stared at the two pearls of sticky, fragrant balsam. He knew the desert is not the quiet place city-dwellers believe. The desert opens the ear. Caravans were bedlam even in the muted sand. Below the level of cranky camels, braying donkeys, and noisome drovers, the cargoes of metal, mineral, and cloth murmured and pushed among themselves in leather packs.

Balsam was more valuable than frankincense and myrrh. Frankincense spoke of possibility. "Imagine this...," Frankincense hissed, like the satan himself. Myrrh could not mute her deathly aroma until some perfumer compounded it with another spice, transforming her keening death march to a dance of good harvests, feasts, stone altars, flutes, drums, and harps.

The balsam plant thrived in arid places, but the most beautiful of aromas was not found in its little berries. It was in her bark. Slice open the bark, then quickly capture the bleeding sap. The tacky resin dries with a sigh into hard nuggets easily transported. Light burden, heavy profit. Tiny balsam drops sang above the camel stink, "Rich! Rich!"

Tzakhi valued balsam. It was a precious plant, aggressively guarded by the southern peoples who cultivated it in places like Sheba. His stepmother Shira would make good use of it. He sniffed the two pieces of resin to see if the merchant was a cheat as well as a donkey-beater. No. It was real, not fake gum resin to fool a boy into dragging half-dead donkeys to a death wadi.

The smell of balsam was rare to most Israelites, but Tzakhi lived in the Tamar fortress, an ancient stopover for caravans from the East. Its gushing oasis spring offered abundant water, and Tzakhi enjoyed the large jujube and tamarisk trees that gave rare full shade from the sun.

Scattered acacia trees in the wilderness offered an illusion of shade, but the sun's persistent arrows shot through the acacia's twisted little branches, fine needles, and coiled bean pods. Huge desert lizards, the *khardons*, burrowed deep into the earth beneath the acacias to shelter from the sweltering midday sun.

Tzakhi dropped the two resin pearls into his pouch, ignoring Ben-Shimi, which most people did. The sun had crawled over the Moabite mountains to the East, and Tzakhi needed to walk to the Chatzeva height and ascend to its flat top. His father Nachshon was overseeing the furnace atop the mountain. The Arava winds raged constantly atop the *givah*, making it a perfect place to super-heat the furnace to temperatures needed to melt the copper and iron ore from Melekh[7] Shlomo's mines. The Chatzeva furnace never required a bellows to raise its temperature like the furnaces of Feynan or Timna.

Tzakhi's father turned the copper and iron ore into oxhorn-shaped ingots for oxcarts to transport to Yerushalayim,[8] Yaffo, Ash-

---

7 king, King Solomon
8 Jerusalem

dod, Egypt, Be'er Sheva, and even Tyre and Sidon. Armorers mixed copper with tin, an even rarer metal brought from the far north, then used it to make bronze. Tzakhi's father always left their house long before sunup with his two military bodyguards to ascend the mountain in the dark or to visit the southern furnaces in Timna.

The coals of the furnace only cooled on Shabbat and during the high holy days. Each workday morning, his father stirred and arranged the coals expertly and assigned work. A master metal-worker like his father was so valuable that he was guarded at all times to prevent him from being kidnapped.

If Ben-Shimi had been more interested in manning his post, he'd have involved himself in the spice dealer's dilemma. He could have asked a few questions to find out how a minimally-competent donkey-beater made it this far in a caravan, even if the answer was that he was just the merchant and his drover fell ill and was left behind.

Rival kingdoms looking for secrets to manufacturing stronger tools and weapons always sought opportunities to steal from the alliance of Egyptians and Israelites. The secret of forging newer weapons of iron drew spies from far countries. Tzakhi never worried too much about his abba being kidnapped for his skill, though. Tamar was one of the strongest fortresses in the South.

Tzakhi was not yet valuable to Israel's king, Melekh Shlomo, but he would pass into the fires as an apprentice when he turned thirteen. He had no idea how to stop it. Tzakhi hated the fires. Abba said he might let him grow an extra year before taking him on his first pilgrimage to Yerushalayim for a *chag*. A chag was a pilgrimage feast that marked a boy's transition to adult obligations. For now, every morning Tzakhi carried the midday meal to the Chatzeva workers and did little jobs around the fortress.

Today's job wasn't so little, but it was going from sad to worse.

CHAPTER THREE

The fallen donkey's foal approached and nuzzled her dam's long ears, but the donkey didn't move. Abba wouldn't wonder where he was until mid-morning because he'd assume Tzakhi found work among the departing caravan or for one of Melekh Shlomo's soldiers who guarded the fortress.

What to do with these two dying donkeys? The holy scroll of the Torah commanded an Israelite to help a fallen donkey to its feet, but it had no clear instruction on what act of mercy to do if the donkey couldn't rise at all. Ben-Shimi had stuck his spear in the sand. Now he cracked pistachio nuts, still watching, glad for some amusement.

Tzakhi walked to the fallen donkey, and her foal shied away. "Smart girl," said Tzakhi. The scrawny foal looked like a moving dark brown bag of acacia sticks.

He knelt and stroked the short mane straggling up from the dam's neck. For a few minutes, Tzakhi just spoke to her, massaging the line of dark hair that formed a cross down the donkey's neck and spine, its crossbar across her shoulders. HaShem[9] drew with a Divine stylus the best place to fasten a donkey's burden.

---

9   God

Tzakhi knew donkeys liked the soft spot behind their long ears scratched. He'd seen them do some acrobatic three-legged feats to scratch there with a hind hoof like a dog. Gently at first, Tzakhi moved the halter and rubbed behind the old girl's ears. She had scars and patches of missing hair, signs of a hard life. After a few more minutes, the donkey's ears moved, and then her muzzle lifted a few inches from the earth.

"That's a girl," said Tzakhi. He dug into his cloth shoulder-bag and took out his lunch: some flat bread his stepmother Shira cooked, a bit of goat cheese, a cluster of dates, and dried *kokhava* leaves to make broth. Tzakhi separated a sweet date and held it to the donkey's lips. At first, she was motionless, as if wondering whether it was a trick to make her care more about living than about simply letting her life-light go out in this powdery sand filled with camel dung. "Go ahead, girl," said Tzakhi.

The soft gray lips nibbled at the date, working around it, testing it, and at last she took it and chewed. She worked it in her mouth for a long time, but then she dropped it to the ground, soggy and torn. This gave Tzakhi an idea.

Cringing a little at the thought of the salivary slime inside, he slipped his hand into the side of the donkey's mouth. In the soft, empty gum space between the front and back teeth, he gripped her tongue firmly and pulled it out the side of her mouth. She opened her mouth, instinctively knowing she'd bite her own tongue if she bit down.

With his other hand, Tzakhi explored the back teeth until he found it. It was a loose, abscessed tooth. The donkey pulled back when he touched the inflamed gums around it with his fingers. Tzakhi hung on to her tongue, but with his other hand he explored the area of the donkey's lower jaw beneath the tooth. There it was, concealed by her shaggy hair. The infection had pushed below her jaw and a huge lump of pus protruded.

Tzakhi didn't have the right tools, but he knew who did. Melekh Shlomo's soldiers had a physician who could treat both people and animals. More than once Tzakhi had seen the physician pull a man's tooth or a horse's with an equal lack of compassion.

The physician could pull the tooth and drain the abscess. A contribution to the vital work of the fortress. Once the donkey could eat and her body was rid of infection, she'd fatten up and be fine.

And that's how Tzakhi acquired two donkeys and two pearls of balsam when he was twelve. Treasures drawn from the Arava's sandy earth. *"So long ago, so long ago,"* sang Tzakhi's mother as he fell asleep.

There was a man of the earth, a man of the sea.
The wolves sang to the man, they taught him the ways of the earth.
Then the earth returned the man to the sea,
Returned him to the sons of man.
So long ago, so long ago.

CHAPTER FOUR

The donkey wasn't that old, said the physician. Maybe only seven or eight, judging from the rest of her teeth. It took a few weeks of treating the abscess so it would continue draining infection from the incision, but she was able to eat immediately after the physician removed the tooth. Tzakhi made a soft mash of dried grape skins and barley grain mixed with warm water for her twice per day, and instead of the rough barley hay, the donkey nibbled on rich grass hay Tzakhi bartered from the royal stable steward.

The steward brought in hay on oxcarts from the terraced farms of the Negev and north of Be'er Sheva in spring and summer, and from Edom and the southern outpost of Yotvata in winter. Hay was precious. Good grass could not grow in the salty sand of the Arava.

Later, it would be okay to feed the donkey cheap barley straw, but there was no telling how long it had been since she'd been able to eat with the bad tooth. She needed the less fibrous, more nutritious hay. Camel milk, dates, and more soft grapeskin and barley mash for the foal supplemented the little milk her dam produced.

Tzakhi paid for the donkeys' fodder by agreeing to shovel horse dung twice per day. Animal dung helped to fuel the furnace fire. It was sweaty, stinking work for most people, but Tzakhi didn't mind shoveling the heavy horse apples onto the wooden sled. He liked horses. A lot. The soldiers let him ride frequently, and he'd been riding them bareback in the sand around the fortress since he could hold a halter-rope.

His secret dream was to train horses for Melekh Shlomo. He'd learned horsemanship from the Israelite soldiers and even visiting Egyptian soldiers. The Egyptian mounts were high-strung, difficult to handle, but swift on the desert sand.

Tzakhi named the donkey Baka. *Balsam.*

The tiny donkey foal overcame her shyness when Tzakhi offered her a sticky date. The little girl had to be hungry, for her dam's udder wasn't full like it should be. Her new teeth were just pushing through, so Tzakhi mashed the sticky date with his hands, and she licked it, sucking his fingers with her little pink tongue until it was all gone. "Matukah," Tzakhi named her. *Sweetie.* She liked the sweet stuff.

As the foal grew over the year, Tzakhi found Matukah didn't bray. She never made a noise. Most donkeys could bray louder than any shofar or trumpet on the Day of Trumpets, but not Matukah. Maybe in those early weeks of limited milk, her body decided it would nourish vital organs instead of her vocal chords.

She would be a small donkey even when full grown, like some of the tiny donkeys bred to fit into low-ceilinged mines. It was a hopeless life. Matukah wasn't hopeless, though. She was indeed a smart girl, and Tzakhi would train her to do more useful things for the fortress. There was hope for her. Tzakhi had been bred for the fires, but he wasn't smart enough to escape them. Soon, he would go with Abba to Yerushalayim for the Feast of Sukkot. After that, hope was gone.

CHAPTER FIVE

Although he dreaded the smelting fires he'd serve afterward, Tzakhi still dreamed of going to Yerushalayim to see the wonders of Melekh Shlomo's world-famous import trade and Temple. He supposed that living on a major trade route had educated him in lots of things, though. You could figure out a lot about people by what they wanted to buy or sell. Every boy usually went to Yerushalayim for one of the three yearly pilgrimage feasts at about the age of twelve or thirteen. It was a rite of passage after which boys would be expected to learn a trade.

As much as Tzakhi wanted to see the splendor of Yerushalayim, the last thing he wanted was his father's trade. He wanted to be a mounted scout or soldier. Captain Avidan had taught him all the skills of an expert desert tracker and fighter, and Avidan said Tzakhi was a natural horseman.

Melekh Shlomo imported purebred horses from Egypt to pull his chariots. They were small and light, nervous and fleet. The king crossbred them with a heavier Hittite breed to combine their speed and desert hardiness with durability. It was these horses the cavalry at Tamar rode.

There were only two divisions, each with ten mounted soldiers, but a hundred foot-soldiers were stationed at the fortress at all times. They protected the furnace, escorted shipments, collected taxes from passing caravans who had to stop for water, and patrolled for bandits.

The vulnerable times for the fortress were when the escort detachments were deployed. Tamar was one of the few places with a large royal treasury. This was necessary to manage the tax income, military wages, and mine-worker wages. It was also where the port city of Etzion-Geber could be re-supplied with coin to purchase from the great merchant ships docking there or to fund one of Melekh Shlomo's ships departing to search for precious cargoes abroad.

When the tax money was escorted to Yerushalayim, an advance troop of fifty infantry soldiers scouted the road skirting the Salt Sea, clearing the route of any bandits, and one detachment of horse soldiers followed, protecting the money. Only fifty infantry soldiers were left to guard the fortress, the furnace, and the inter-secting roads to the King's Highway.

Tzakhi only mentioned his dream to his father once. His father grunted dismissively. Their family had worked the copper furnaces since the time of Yehoshua...even before. His father was descended from a son of Betzalel, who'd overseen the metalwork of the Israelite Tabernacle in the time of Moshe.[10]

Every male descendant of Betzalel learned the mining and forging of copper in the Arava wilderness of Judea, even making alliances with Midianites, Moabites, Egyptians, Kenites, and Edomites in times of war or political upheaval in Canaan.

In war, a descendant of Betzalel might be captured, but never killed. Their knowledge was too precious to be lost. Most recently, Melekh Shlomo sent a master craftsman, Khiram of Tyre, to Tamar

---

10 Moses

to exchange knowledge of bronze and iron working techniques with Tzakhi's abba.

As keepers of the metalworking skills and secrets, the House of Nachshon had largely escaped bloody battles for control of the mines. No matter who controlled the mines, they wanted expert miners and smelters to produce the valuable copper for export and weapons.

Like the Kenites, a clan of friendly Midianites, a master metalworker merely changed lords when his tribe or nation lost a battle or war. Superior metalworking assured a king the most advanced spears, arrowheads, swords, and daggers.

When it came to the various Edomite, Moabite, Midianite, and Egyptian conquerors of the mines, they didn't care which god their expert craftsmen worshiped. Not until Melekh David had anyone cared or bothered to clear out the many incense altars from the fortress. Only then did the administrators demand that no foreign altars be erected inside the Tamar fortress walls.

Tzakhi had no interest in the mines or mountaintop furnaces, though. He loved the desert and its creatures. He could handle camels and donkeys better than most of the drovers, and he could sit a horse as well as the king's riders, even handle a chariot in soft sand. Tzakhi listened to an animal like he listened to the caravan merchants in trade. Each had its own language and personality. You simply gave each one a little of what it wanted in order to reap the reward of cooperation or obedience.

So far, Tzakhi had not figured out how to make changing his future occupation something his father wanted. If his abba didn't want it, he'd never permit it. Outside of work, Tzakhi's abba was almost as silent as his occupation, *charash*. A *charash* was someone who worked in metal, but it also meant someone without the power of speech. From ancient times, the *charashim* were close-mouthed about their craft, divulging secrets only to the reigning power.

The months passed, and Tzakhi turned thirteen years old. He knew he would go with his abba to the Feast of Sukkot in Yerushalayim, the time when all his brothers...except one...entered his abba's trade as an apprentice. One exception gave him hope. His brother Salmah was sent north two years ago, not long after his hair began to streak with silver.

"Too much like his mother," was the only explanation Tzakhi received from his father when Abba returned from the Yerushalayim pilgrimage without Salmah. Salmah had turned thirteen, and it was his first pilgrimage to the City of David. "I sent him away before the Arava swallowed him."

"So where is he?" Tzakhi had asked.

"He went to the school of the prophets at Beit El," said Abba. "He can play his little flute to his heart's content there."

The school of the prophets. Tzakhi had heard of them because he'd heard of almost everything from the caravans. There were bands of musicians who played instruments, learned Torah, and prophesied. They were mystics, but also masters of the words of Moshe.

"Too much like his mother." Salmah was dreamy, frequently alone in the wilderness with his flute. He could watch a lizard under an acacia tree or salt bush for hours, even make pets of them. Tzakhi followed Salmah one time, tracking him to the Ein Tzin wadi. It was not far from Scorpions' Ascent, the winding mountain trail the caravans used.

By the time he'd caught up to him, Salmah was sitting among the gurgling desert springs on a rock. It was nearly twilight, and a full moon hung low above the mountains in the wadi. Salmah played his flute softly, and a pack of wolves sat in a semicircle before him.

Tzakhi listened to the haunting tones, unsure what to do, but Salmah was not afraid. Eventually, Salmah stood, and Tzakhi held his breath. Salmah switched to a merry tune, an ancient song from the wilderness wandering of their ancestors. He played it with all its quick rhythm, and he danced in place while he played.

The wolves, too, stood, and played around his feet, tumbling, bowing, wrestling, and grinning at one another to the beat. It was like a dream, and Tzakhi could only watch as his brother and the wolves gamboled to the song:

> *The wilderness and the desert will be glad,*
> *And the Arava will rejoice and blossom like the crocus.*
> *It will blossom abundantly and rejoice with rejoicing and*
> *shouts of joy.*[11]

When Salmah followed with a mournful psalm of David, the wolves halted their white-toothed dancing, and they sat again. One by one, they raised their voices to the moon, howling until every hair stood on Tzakhi's body. The long howls reverberated through the wadi, echoing, crashing, flooding through the sand and rock like a winter flood sweeping away all signs of life and death. Maybe Melekh David had done the same before he became king, playing his harp with the ancestors of this very pack.

The school of the prophets. Tzakhi had no such talent as to charm wolves with a flute, but he could coax a donkey or horse into just about anything. Maybe Salmah could advise him on how to approach the topic with his father again if they met in Yerusha-

---

11 Isaiah 35:1

layim at the feast. It was the last chance for the other silver-haired son to escape the apprenticeship of bronze fire.

So long ago, so long ago.
The man took a wife from the sons of the sea
A daughter of blue and green and sand.
Then fire sprang from the earth,
The fire fell down from the sky so black.
The man and his wife sailed the blue and green,
And so their children of earth and sea and sand.
So long ago, so long ago.

CHAPTER SIX

After the Day of Trumpets, the Feast of Sukkot approached, and Tzakhi's older brothers trickled in from Timna, Feynan, Eilat, and Etzion-Geber. They would observe the solemn day of fasting, Yom HaKippurim, together, then journey up to Yerushalayim.

Tzakhi was summoned inside their house by Uri, who just finished his meeting with Abba. Abba and Elad sat in the inside court of their stone house, the work area for a hundred tasks. They reclined on cushions, holding cool cups of barley beer brewed by Egyptians at Timna. Each Sukkot, Elad brought a large jug of the honeyed brew, and they buried it in the cool, shady sand of a corner of the house. The two of them sat in a nook away from where the women were working.

Shira looked up when Tzakhi walked past, and she gave him an encouraging smile amidst the bustle of food preparation. "*B'chatzlekha*," she mouthed to him. *Good success.*

She'd hired an extra servant while the brothers were there because she was unused to cooking for more than a few people. Tzakhi's sisters-in-law pitched in, too, feeding the voracious appetites of Nachshon's red-headed clan. While Tzakhi's older brothers built a sukkah onto the shadier north side of the house, the women were constantly preparing food, packing, and re-packing provisions for the pilgrimage to Yerushalayim.

One by one today, Abba would call in his sons, starting with the oldest, to review their progress since Abba's last visit to their work sites. They would also talk about their families. In years past, Tzakhi had only been a part of these conversations in passing, but today, he was invited to sit last.

Today he would find out which fire he would serve. Smelting? Refining? Copper? Iron?

Tzakhi wasn't sure what beer tasted like, but he suspected the news would go down better with a cup. Abba gestured to him to sit with him and Elad. He didn't offer a cup of the Egyptian beer.

"You are now of the age to make pilgrimage to Yerushalayim," said Abba.

"*Ken*,[12] Abba," said Tzakhi.

"And we must determine the best place for you to apprentice," Abba added.

So no small talk for Tzakhi. Tzakhi had no wife or children to tell about. No production problems or successes. He'd not even earned a place in the conversation yet.

In disappointment too great to embrace, Tzakhi fixed his eyes on the low wooden table, focused on a plate of dates and almonds, then allowed them to lose focus. Somehow the blur helped him retreat from what he didn't want to hear.

"You're still small," Abba said. "You need a little more weight to bear the work at Timna, and every son must begin there to learn metal from where it is dug. Elad was much stronger at the same age. You do well working around Tamar. Lifting the packs has made your arms strong, but not enough. You may never grow as

---

12 "Yes."

sturdy as your brothers, and if not, then later you can learn with Barzillai or Ovadyah the administrative side of things. You'll not join us on the pilgrimage this year, but you do need to fast with us on the holy day of Yom HaKippurim. Wait another year, and I'll ask Shira to start feeding you more."

Fed more? Like a calf fattened to slaughter for a feast? Yet, Tzakhi relaxed and focused his eyes, pulling himself back into the room. Relief, oh, cool relief better than an Egyptian beer could possibly provide. Another year. "*Ken*, Abba," said Tzakhi.

Elad, who was forever serious, smiled at him a little. The release from constant worry must have shown on Tzakhi's face.

His relief was clouded by the one disappointment. He wouldn't be able to see Salmah. Maybe Salmah would sense how much he missed him. Maybe Salmah would be glad he was held back from the fires for a little longer. Maybe Salmah would pray to HaShem for him in the Holy Temple.

Abba sipped from his cup. "Anything you want to say or ask, Tzakhi?"

"Please tell Salmah '*Chag sameach*,'"[13] said Tzakhi simply. He was afraid Abba would find it too sentimental, unmanly, if he said to tell Salmah how much he missed him.

Abba and Elad both nodded at his request. Tzakhi could see Abba was preparing Elad to take over. Elad was like Abba's shadow in dedication to the work and even in personality. "Go help your brothers build the sukkah," said Abba. "This will be your last year to stay behind, so I expect you to watch over everyone while we're gone. Help the women when they need it, and take a firm hand with the boys. Make sure they are not rough with the girls, *b'seder*?"

---

13 Happy holiday

"B'seder," agreed Tzakhi. He stood and walked into the bright sunlight.

Most of his brothers, their wives, and children assembled after The Day of Trumpets at Abba's house in Tamar before his brothers made the journey together up to Yerushalayim. The ones who worked north in the verdant Yarden Valley would meet them in the Holy City. Tzakhi always enjoyed the reunion because his older brothers alternately teased and doted on him as the youngest. His meeting with Abba was over, so he could now enjoy the good-natured chaos of building the sukkah.

The flimsy outdoor shelter was propped up with acacia poles and shaded by palm fronds. Once set, palm fronds would be worked into the cross supports to form the walls. It always took longer to build than it should because each brother was accustomed to giving orders, not to taking them. The result was not a sturdier hut, but one requiring frequent repair during the seven days of Sukkot.

"I would rather be preparing food with the women," complained Uri, who was tired of holding a corner support pole. It was only shallowly dug into the sand, which couldn't hold it. Natan, who was a bit surly on the best of days, was kneeling, alternately digging deeper into the sand and working the pole downward. Tzakhi knew from experience the sand wouldn't stabilize the pole. The dug sand was as loose as powder, and it would offer no resistance when back-filled into the hole.

Natan and Uri should know that, too. They both grew up here and had helped build the sukkah since they were boys. It was strange how a few years of working with the unbending copper and iron could deceive you into thinking the Arava sand wouldn't shift. "I'll bring the sandbags," said Tzakhi. He'd prepared them weeks before, pouring loose sand into rough cloth bags that could turn the powder into the strength of rocks.

"You're just now telling us you have sandbags?" roared Natan.

"It's just now his problem instead of yours," Uri pointed out.

"They're lined up on the side of the house," said Tzakhi. "I didn't think you'd miss them."

Natan cast him a look of pure disgust through the pale sand-powder mask coating the upper part of his face.

Uri howled with laughter. "Little Tzakhi has big attitude! *Metzach nechusha!*"

Natan placed his hands on his thighs and looked up. Sweat dripped from his face into his wiry red beard, leaving rivulets through the coating of sand. Maybe the sweat was the only thing keeping his beard from catching fire. It was a thought Tzakhi kept to himself. Wordlessly, Natan abandoned his work and went to the other corner to help Ovadyah and Barzillai.

Within a few minutes, Tzakhi was filling around the re-dug and re-packed hole with bags of sand to stabilize it.

He and Uri finished, then went to help secure the opposite corner, which was no closer to being set than when they started. Ovadyah had given up and was holding one of Elad's boys on his shoulders while he tied some branches across the roof. It wasn't going well because the corner support was being constantly wrestled back and forth by Natan and Pinchas.

They were twins, and equally hot-headed with each other as well as anyone else who disrupted their way of doing things. Finally, they stood back and analyzed their work, which was supported now by sandbags. Tzakhi could tell they hadn't sunk the pole deep enough, and the sandbags wouldn't hold.

"At least put a shade up there while we work," said Barzillai, who was leaning on his crutch and fastening a cross-support pole.

"You get a few weeks away from the furnace, and you still want to sweat like donkeys."

Pinchas retorted, "Speaking of donkeys, why don't you carry your..."

Barzillai tapped on the corner pole with his crutch. It collapsed.

The roof frame fell down on all of them.

Tzakhi couldn't help it. He started laughing. Maybe it was the relief of not being apprenticed. Maybe it was the irony of the most skilled metalworkers in Israel being totally incompetent at building a simple hut. He pushed away the acacia poles fallen on the ground around him. One by one, his brothers started laughing, too, lifting and pushing away the tangle. None of them could stop, either, even Pinchas and Natan. They laughed so loudly that Abba, Elad, and the women and children came to see what the matter was. Then they, too, started laughing at the wreck of a sukkah.

Like the sukkah-building, the house was as boisterous as a large caravan until the men of Tamar left along with the Nachshon clan, riding horses, donkeys, and mules north. Afterward, the women and girls slept in the house, and the boys slept in the sukkah at night even before the feast started. Although the men traveled in the summer at the Shavuot feast and in the spring for Pesach, Sukkot was the most fun because of the many meals in the sukkah. As his older brothers had doted on him, so Tzakhi could dote on his nieces and nephews after the men were gone.

His stepmother Shira usually added the best spices to her dishes for Shabbat, and the aromas drove the remaining soldiers of the Tamar fortress fairly mad with envy. During Sukkot, every meal was Shabbat-best. Although fresh fruits and vegetables were almost non-existent in the Arava desert in summer, not even the wealthiest families in Yerushalayim enjoyed the steady supply of aromatics along the Spice Trail like Tamar. Shira generously shared their meals with the few soldiers stationed there during the feast.

Shira was his stepmother, but she was not much older than Tzakhi. She turned the dried fruits and vegetables into delicious warm pots of spiced meats and sweet breads. It hadn't taken her long to learn what foods and spices were friends on the tongue.

After his own mother died, may her memory be for blessing, Tzakhi spent many Shabbats eating plain, cold food in the barracks with the soldiers until his father remarried. For all his abba's skill with fire, he'd never learned to cook. He preferred to eat with the soldiers than to hire an additional servant. Shira's spices and her kindness had made their house warm again.

In spite of all the work of the feasts, Tzakhi could tell Shira also enjoyed the big family gathering and female company. She'd grown up among females in a palace of women, so she was at home with the higher-pitched chatter. Tamar was usually a place of rough male voices, but not during the feasts.

When Abba returned from the Feast in Yerushalayim, he did not mention seeing Salmah at all. For many months after the feast, Tzakhi's thoughts turned to Salmah, hoping his brother could hear his silent words, trying to hear any words Salmah might be saying back to him. His days of sleeping in the sukkah at Tamar with the boys were over. There was only one thing left he could do if he wanted to feel close to Salmah.

CHAPTER SEVEN

Almost a year later, two-year-old Matukah munched barley in the near-darkness of her small, rock shelter. Only a clay oil lamp illuminated the three-sided stone hut Tzakhi had thatched with tamarisk and palm branches. The moon lingered in the early-morning sky, but the moon was moody. She only offered to help Tzakhi for around a week at mid-month. When the moon was full, she couldn't hide her bloated, white sheen.

Like the Arava desert where Tzakhi lived, the moon's appearance was pocked, maybe with the same kind of craters and wadis hiding the seashells he loved to pluck from the sand and rock. Maybe it had holes in its white earth that sometimes spewed fire like the legend in his mother's song.

Tzakhi's fingers worked the ropes around the two great baskets sticking out from the donkey's sides like reed wings. He secured the baskets for the trip up the Chatzeva mountain to carry midday rations. His father was already there, stirring coals in the great furnace, and Baka was on her way with a load of firewood.

"Hurry, Matukah," said Tzakhi to the donkey, and she paused in her loud chewing. She was a funny donkey. Matukah didn't have the hopeless look of the caravan donkeys who passed through the Tamar fortress.

Although she never brayed, Matukah listened attentively when Tzakhi talked. She was small, but smart. She'd already learned to carry the light food burdens. Matukah would return to the water trough when Tzakhi told her, "*Lekhi habayitah, Matukah.*" Like her dam, he'd trained her to be an oversized carrier pigeon. The administrators used pigeons and rock doves to send and receive messages all the way to Yerushalayim, Be'er Sheva, and Etzion-Geber.

While he waited for Matukah to finish her breakfast, Tzakhi curried her coarse, chestnut coat. Her sire must have been chestnut because Baka was a dun. Tzakhi thought about Abba's hair color, which was the color of the ingots separated from the copper slag, bright red. Red like the mountains of Edom where he'd spent his life firing copper ore for weapons to fill the armories of Egypt and Israel. He kept the trade ships moving from Etzion-Geber to Tyre.

Tzakhi's mother had a fairer complexion, but her eyes were green and her hair was darkest black with silver streaks. Both Tzakhi and his only full brother Salmah developed similar streaks of silver in their black hair, and their eyes were green as well. Rather than endure the soldiers' sly jokes about his father's fiery copper hair and his own silver streaks, Tzakhi wore his turban whenever he was outdoors. Tzakhi wasn't sure where his mother was from. She never said. She only said that she was from the tribe of Benjamin.

Salmah didn't know, either. It was as if their mother sprouted like a bright desert crocus in winter, only to disappear into the dust long before spring. Tzakhi felt fortunate, though. Two of his older brothers, the twins Pinchas and Natan, had never met their mother, who died after giving birth.

Tzakhi could frequently distinguish among the Israelite tribes by their Hebrew dialect and physical features, but his mother and

Salmah didn't really fit the mold. Although Tzakhi was a bit sturdier than Salmah at the same age, he was still of smaller build than all his half-brothers. He wondered if his abba ever noticed that like Salmah, Tzakhi wasn't really built for the furnace. He was built like a horse soldier, not tall or short, but wiry with long, slim legs.

After he walked Matukah to the trailhead and saw her amble reliably up the trail to the furnace atop the givah, Tzakhi turned toward his house. Maybe Shira could help him sort out what to do. She would have warmed some flatbread over the coals and spread it with date honey, and there would be a bowl of toasted pistachios or almonds. He'd better enjoy it now. Once he was sent to a mining camp, he'd be eating cold workers' rations for breakfast every day.

So long ago, so long ago.
A family of earth and sea and sand sailed to Egypt
A family with eyes of wolves, with eyes of the sea.
In Egypt also were wolves, also lions and serpents
And in Egypt were oxen and donkeys and deer.
So long ago, so long ago.

CHAPTER EIGHT

Shira wasn't at her best in the morning. She said only the servants stirred before dawn in the women's quarters of the palace. Now she was married, she was a servant, too. She had to wake and rise with Abba to prepare him a small meal for breakfast. Tzakhi had heard her bumbling through the lighting of lamps, stirring of coals, and assembling the meal her first few months at Tamar. He asked her how it felt to go from being served to serving.

Shira smiled at the memory of her errors. "Fortunately, Tzakhi, your abba's temperament doesn't match his red hair. He rarely raises his voice around women, and he never raises it to me. Perhaps it is a discipline he learned when the fiery sparks from the furnaces lit on his skin. You know he had one of the women from the tents come teach me cooking and how to manage the house. That was very intelligent and kind of him."

"True," said Tzakhi.

When he worked a furnace, Abba stripped to only short, close-fitting breeches, a leather apron, and a long-sided leather cap so his clothes and hair would not catch fire from the popping sparks. His broad body was covered with tiny burn scars, and he simply ignored the orange brands when they flew up. There was an especially bad set of scars on his forearms. Unlike most men his age who grew long beards, Nachshon had to keep his short, and still there were patches of nappy, burned, red hair.

Tzakhi's half-brothers worked at every level of production. They started in the mines, then with the on-site smelting, and then to the refining camps. One brother, Barzillai, had been injured by a rock fall and limped badly. He supervised distribution from the port of Etzion-Geber.

Once per year, in the heat of the summer that competed with the furnaces, Nachshon took Tzakhi with him to Etzion-Geber. He was allowed a few weeks of swimming in the sapphire waters while his father went over business with Uri, Barzillai, and various officials. Abba was kind, but in the end, he and his sons always produced the rows of tidy, oxhorn-shaped ingots.

Shira continued, "The desert is hard on family life for everyone, but it's especially lonely in Tamar for a woman. We must be careful when the caravans are here. Those men are very...rough."

"You have guards," said Tzakhi. Nachshon's personal detail of four soldiers ensured the family was not harmed, freeing Abba to travel when necessary. Two soldiers guarded Abba at all times, even two on the night watch, and two more took turns guarding Shira from lecherous travelers or soldiers during the day.

Tzakhi was free to roam, and for this he was glad. The commanders, professional soldiers, and tax administrators were allowed the luxury of having their families at Tamar, but conscripted foot soldiers worked three months at a time and then returned home when the next rotation took their places. They weren't born wilderness men.

Shira said, "Yes, I have guards. Guards watch my every move when I step foot out of the house. Tzakhi, you have ten older brothers from your abba's first three wives, each of whom died in childbirth or not many years after. Maybe you should be glad to go to the mines. It's the first step out of servitude. You'll progress, maybe even learn the secrets of iron-casting or go to the Yarden Valley clay fields to cast bronze for my father. It's lush and beautiful there. You'll start a family of your own."

"Family," echoed Tzakhi faintly, feeling a little wave of sadness. It was not as strong as the first year after Ima died, but he still missed her. Tzakhi's mother had borne Salmah and Tzakhi, lived precariously, then succumbed to a fever. Childbirth was dangerous, but Abba merely found a new wife each time to take care of his sons. Yes, the desert swallowed the weak. The young replaced them. All trails led to the fires from this house.

"You were very young when you arrived here," said Tzakhi.

"Yes," said Shira. "And pampered. Shielded from much of public life. It is not much different here. Just harder."

Tzakhi wasn't sure how the marriages were contracted, but Shira had shown up in a caravan on a camel accompanied by Melekh Shlomo's steward. Her arrival was also accompanied by five camels loaded with gifts from dried foodstuff to copper pots. She was from the tribe of Judah, a daughter of one of Melekh Shlomo's concubines. Shira was a gift of appreciation to Nachshon from the king. Her age surprised Tzakhi when she removed the veil shielding her from the desert sand. She was only fourteen then, four years older than Tzakhi.

The first few months were hard on the girl, who'd grown up in an extended part of Melekh Shlomo's palace only to be dropped off in Tamar's howling wilderness to marry a large, red-haired man who smelled of smoke and slag, a man who shaved his hair frequently to avoid catching it on fire.

"I tried to help you," said Tzakhi. He had tried hard to help Shira, sad that a girl could be given as a piece of property, but also glad to have more company in the big stone house, especially someone close to his age. Salmah disappeared often, and their older brothers were all either working at the Timna furnaces or apprenticed to the Jordan Valley smiths who turned tin and copper into bronze weapons or vessels for use in the Temple and palace.

"Shira?"

"Yes?"

"Do you think you...maybe...?"

"Maybe what, Tzakhi,?"

"You gave up."

"Gave up what?"

Tzakhi said, "You know, when you married my abba. You were a princess..."

"No, Tzakhi. The children of concubines are not princes or princesses. Apparently, that stopped with our father Ya'akov's concubines. We're just glorified servants to serve our abba's strategic purposes, nothing more. The boys serve in the government or military, and the girls become servants to the royals of other nations or are given as gifts," said Shira.

Tzakhi knew this was true because he heard everything from the caravans. He stayed silent rather than make the situation harsh. And his own position was little better than hers.

"Go ahead, ask me," said Shira more gently. "What did I give up?"

"When you first came here, you were..."

"...scared," Shira finished for him.

"Yes," said Tzakhi. "But kind of disconnected. Like you couldn't believe you were here and you were waiting for another caravan to take you back to Yerushalayim."

"True," said Shira. "A caravan that will never come."

"But after a few months, it seemed like you gave up. You started learning your way around the fortress, learning how to cook with the foods we have here, how to serve Abba and work around his schedule. It doesn't seem like you want anything anymore other than to just get through each day," said Tzakhi.

"You were good to me," said Shira. "You were like my little brother. I missed him a lot. It made it easier to accept what I had to be. And what else is there other than to just get through each day, at least for a woman?"

"But what if you didn't want to just give up?" asked Tzakhi. "What if you wanted something different than what Abba made you do?"

"Whatever else would I want, Tzakhi?"

"I don't know. Maybe to make nice pottery."

"That's what the Midianites do, Tzakhi. No one needs more nice pottery."

"Or have a regular business with the caravan. You buy the Midianite pottery and the new juglets from the North, make balms and unguents to put in them, and I sell it all to the caravans. And you make jewelry from the seashells and copper and turquoise I bring you. You dry the tea from the *kokhava* leaves I collect in winter, and I sell it for you. You learned from the Midianite women, and you are clever. Why not make a real business?"

Shira smiled. "The ointments and jewelry keep me busy while your abba is gone, Tzakhi. A clever woman is an asset only to herself."

"No, I mean..."

"Just come out with it, Tzakhi. I'm not good at your mind games. You've practiced too long haggling with the camel and donkey drovers."

"I don't want to be a charash. I want to train horses for the king. Or scout for the army. Anything but watching slaves pound copper and iron from rocks to put in the fires."

Shira didn't respond, so Tzakhi continued, "I've learned everything the Israelite soldiers know, and I've learned from the

Dedanite horse traders and Egyptian chariot drivers...even from the riders from across The River who ride the Caspian horses."

Kindly, Shira didn't remind him Abba would never permit it. Instead, she said, "The king's breeding stables are in the North where there's lots of pasturage and grain fields, at Har Meggido. You like it here in the Arava."

As if extending her father's scepter, she handed him a warmed piece of flat bread with goat cheese, minced dates, mint, and cooked grain rolled inside. "I did give up, Tzakhi. It's all a girl can do whether she's the king's daughter or the daughter of a beggar. But Salmah escaped the furnace. Maybe with that wise silver hair of yours, you'll find a way, too."

CHAPTER NINE

Tzakhi plucked his shofar from its peg over his bed mat. The ram's horn hung from a leather strap, which Tzakhi threw over his shoulder. After making sure his water skin was full and he had a few flatbreads and dates thrown in with his flints, he tightened his sandal laces and set off west. The guard at the outer gate gave him a long look. "Where's your donkey?" he asked.

Tzakhi said, "Didn't you see her? Baka took a load of wood and food up to the *givah*." He wished Ben-Shimi were that interested in inspecting the caravans.

"Sure, I saw her," lied the soldier. Ben-Shimi wasn't the most observant of guards. He was more interested in what went on in the tent of an Edomite trader outside the fortress walls. Tzakhi knew what went on in the tent with the women inside. He knew everything from the caravan drovers.

The captain periodically drove away the Edomite when a top official came to visit the mines, but the trader was like a flea on a dog. He was never really gone with his women, gambling games, and occasional slave trading. The Edomite was only absent when he moved his tent to offer his services at the caravansaries in Avdat or Botzra.

Tzakhi had trained Baka to climb the mountain on her own. Once she was loaded with firewood, Tzakhi had only to point her west, and she would slowly walk across the sand and climb the mountain trail to the top. The workers would unload her, feed her a few handfuls of grain Tzakhi had tucked inside the basket, then reload her with what needed to go back to the fortress.

Baka then returned to the fortress, and Tzakhi could find her at the watering trough near the great jujube tree, switching her tail in the shade. If it took too long for someone to give her grain and re-pack her with firewood or unpack her in the evening, she'd bray loudly at the delay. She liked her naps, but she liked the grain and a sweet date she earned at the end of each trip even more.

Today, Tzakhi trusted Baka to find her way home and one of the furnace donkey drovers to unpack her. He set off across the desert toward Ein Tzin, a wadi near the Scorpions' Ascent. Fresh water bubbled from the sand and rocks, making it easier to track the many desert creatures who visited the perpetual springs each night. It was there Tzakhi had seen Salmah charming the wolfpack a few years before.

Abba was gone to the Timna mines, so Tzakhi wouldn't be missed tonight. Shira never questioned him, knowing sometimes Tzakhi slept in the stable if he was tending colicky horses for the soldiers, or sometimes he slept on the rooftop when the nights were warm.

It was dusk when Tzakhi arrived, but his stomach was curiously calm. He found Salmah's white rock and crawled atop it, setting his bag to one side. After a moment of consideration, he pulled his turban from his head, and waves of silver-streaked black hair tumbled to his shoulders like foam on black water during the new moon.

He took several long drinks from his water skin and ran his tongue across his lips. This was the only way he could talk to Salmah. The school of the prophets. A wolf prophet. Tzakhi was no prophet. He was no musician. But he could blow a shofar better than most. Positioning the small end of the curled ram's horn along his lips, Tzakhi blew.

He blew the *tekiah* call, and the sound echoed through the wadi. To make the tekiah, he modulated his breath, and the result was a long, wolf-like howl. After listening for a moment and hearing nothing, Tzakhi repeated the call. Again, nothing. The silence, however, was not a dead one. There was some stirring of energy in the graylight. Maybe it was just the vipers, owls, night hawks, and other creatures of the night getting up to go to work.

Tzakhi had spent time in the desert at night, but not this far from the fortress alone. He sat and counted the stars, checking to see if there were at least three of them. Three would indicate evening had set in, starting a new day. To the west, orange drained out of the sky.

And then there were eyes.

A semicircle of watchful eyes.

The wolves had slipped around the rock, the sound of their big paws muted by the solid rock shelf of the spring. Their eyes glittered at Tzakhi. Was he food like the dead camels and donkeys they tore to pieces before the flash floods washed the bones into the lower basin of the Salt Sea? A large pup approached, stood on his hind legs, and sniffed Tzakhi's sandals. A she-wolf gave a low growl. The pup backed away, wrinkling his lips and showing ivory teeth in apology. Maybe the she-wolf was the pack leader.

There was irony.

Tzakhi held the shofar to his lips and again imitated a long wolf howl. The she-wolf tilted back her head, and her own howl blended with the shofar. The rest of the pack followed suit, flooding the wadi with their night song. Together, Tzakhi and wolves sang, sometimes echoing one another, sometimes together. Far in the distance, howls from another pack answered.

After about twenty minutes, the she-wolf approached, but this time, Tzakhi wasn't afraid. He sat still, cross-legged, but straight. The tawny she-wolf sniffed first the shofar, then Tzakhi's knees before backing away. After a little milling about, some conversation among the long-legged pack, she led them into the darkness of the reeds.

Afterward, Tzakhi used the light of the full moon to follow the game trail back to the Spice Road leading back to the fortress. The pack trailed him for about four thousand *amot*, something he sensed rather than saw. Tzakhi wasn't sure if they were following him like perhaps they followed Salmah, or if they were working up their appetites for him.

So long ago, so long ago.
Children with eyes of the wolf,
Children with eyes of the sea lived in Egypt.
And the children lived with wolves,
The children lived with lions.
Their cubs were pale,
Their cubs were dark.
Cubs of earth,
Cubs of the sea.
So long ago, so long ago.

CHAPTER TEN

The badlands northeast of Tamar helpfully opened inviting jaws, and then closed its victims in an unsolvable maze of wadis. There was not even a parable or a storyteller's tale imagining escape. The Arava lay vast and wide, ready to soak a human or animal into its sands like a drop of water, leaving nothing but leathery parchments of skin and bones to be blown into sand banks and buried.

There was little danger of an enemy approach from the northeast. They would have to find a stealthy approach over the mountains of Moab in the east, through the mines and outposts of the south, or by threading a needle of outposts between Tamar and the Great Sea. Judah in the north was secure.

It was early morning, and Captain Avidan and Tzakhi walked together, skirting the west side of Givat Chatzeva, checking around an empty wadi for animal or human tracks in the sand. It was away from the highways, but a perfect place for robbers to lurk and observe the fortress.

Tzakhi led the captain's powerful mare. She was a special gift from the palace to Avidan. Noa had the refined, regal head of an Egyptian sire and Egyptian speed, yet she had the height and leg power of the heavier Hittite chariot horses. The veins stood out on her deep, blood-bay coat, and her shiny black mane and tail ruffled in the quiet morning wind.

The tracks were the usual ones: hyena, jackal, wolf, leopard, caracal, ibex, porcupine, gazelle, and thin lines of partridge, chukar, and grouse feet. The birds left their light overnight scratchy artistry to be erased soon by the winds. Their tracks looked a lot like Ashuri tablet-writing, messages written with human letters in a bird language.

And then there was something unusual. Hoofprints. The area was concealed by an overhanging rock, and the earth was trampled soft as if animals had stood there for several hours. Avidan went still, scanning the bigger area, then focusing back on the area beneath the overhang. He walked slowly, examining the ground and rock for any more telling signs.

"What kind of horses?" Avidan asked Tzakhi.

"Egyptian," said Tzakhi. "The shape of the hooves is Egyptian-bred. They're light. Probably mares so they won't whinny at other horses or donkeys."

"Riders?"

"Yes," said Tzakhi. "The prints leading up here are heavier. They dismounted here." Tzakhi bent and picked up a sliver of grayish-white date pit. "And stayed long enough to eat."

"Then what?" asked the captain.

Tzakhi silently tracked the faint sandal prints, and Avidan trailed him leading Noa. Although the sandal prints continued past the first tumble of rocks, Tzakhi stopped. He knew the scouting maneuver, and he'd lose the tracks in the fine pebble. He said, "One stayed back holding the horses. Two advanced on foot. One went ahead, cleared the terrain, then the second advanced and cleared to the next hide. I'm not sure where they stopped, but I'm sure they could watch the givah and the fortress from at least four vantage points without being seen during the day."

"Well-done," said Avidan, and Tzakhi smiled inside.

Avidan turned and went back to where the horses would have waited, this time to track from which direction they left. They followed the hoof prints, retracing the steps away from the overhang for a short distance, but the wind had erased the trail. An area of small rock skirted the sand and extended for a distance from the mountain into the desert. Smart. Whoever had spent time watching the top of Givat Chatzeva from this hiding place hadn't bothered to obliterate signs of their presence, but the departure route ensured no one could follow unless he could split into three directions toward the three oases within a reasonable journey.

Tzakhi could see this troubled Avidan. There was no reason for an Egyptian to spy on the furnace activities. The Pharaoh and Melekh Shlomo were allies by covenant. Ashurim from the Great River, maybe? The Ashurim were strong and becoming stronger, rivaling Bavel.

That was one reason for the alliance between Pharaoh and Melekh Shlomo. Both were concerned about the rising power in the northeast. Ashur was controlling much of the trade and taxation of the fertile fields of the Perat[14] and Chiddekkel[15] rivers. Their army was growing, funded by the abundance of growing vassal states.

The traffic on the King's Highway and Spice Routes made it difficult to conceal a small detachment of spies, and the badlands to the northeast were impossible to traverse without being hopelessly lost. If the watchers circled here to the southwest, though,

---

14 Euphrates
15 Tigris

there were many hideouts between Israel and Egypt. This is where the ghosts of the flying scorpion-snake, the *tzirah*, hid. No one had ever seen a dead one or even its bones. Maybe the stinging creatures were unable to die, like a sheid.

Captain Avidan was silent, and when they turned back to the fortress, he nodded to Tzakhi to mount Noa and ride. Avidan did this when he needed to think. Noa modulated her steps to remain by Avidan's side, and after a while, Tzakhi asked Avidan, "Why is this place called Ir Ovot? Does it mean 'city of waterskins,' or 'city of dead spirits'?"

Avidan scanned behind them as he walked before he answered. "It's recorded by Moshe in the Torah. It's prophecy. Words like that have many meanings."

"So both?" asked Tzakhi. The Levite at Tamar had said something vaguely similar.

To this Avidan smiled. "Yes, both. It's always been a caravansary because of the spring, a place to fill dry waterskins, to resurrect a thirsty traveler or a flock of sheep. But it's also a place where the veil is thin. The dead here are waiting, I think. Don't you hear them whisper sometimes?"

Tzakhi's abba would never tolerate such ideas. His world was earth, rock, and fire, forcing the elements into uniform, pure, and useful ingots. Flutes, desert craft, flying serpents, and whispering souls were a waste of time.

"Yes," said Tzakhi. "Not hear them like real sounds, but still something I hear around me. They don't make me afraid."

"No," said Avidan. "They are content. Just waiting here. And such a strange place for them to wait."

"Maybe it's the souls of those who fell in the wilderness journey to the Promised Land," said Tzakhi.

"Never thought of that," said Avidan. "But perhaps. No one has ever found their bones or knows where they were buried. Each time I ride to Ein Tzin, I look for where Miriam of blessed memory may be buried, but nothing stands out."

"Maybe Hashem took her like he took Moshe," said Tzakhi, wondering if somehow Avidan knew of his secret journey there to visit the wolves.

"Maybe," said Avidan. "Don't go to that wadi alone, Tzakhi. Stay between the furnace and the fortress unless you go with a patrol. The spring attracts all sorts of predators, animal and human."

"Yes, sir." That settled it. It wasn't a random caution.

Avidan never seemed to mind Tzakhi's questions like his abba did. "How did you meet Melekh David?" asked Tzakhi.

Avidan absently sharpened the blade of his knife on a piece of leather strap as he walked.

"Before David was melekh, I was a fugitive with my abba," said Avidan. "Abba owed Nahval money. Edomites had stolen many of my father's sheep, and his abba...my *saba*...borrowed money. When Saba died, he left abba with the debt. Abba and his brother agreed they would borrow the money from Nahval of Maon to pay the debt so their *ima*[16] would be clear, and my uncle would take her in his home. A disease ravaged our sheep the following winter, and neither could pay the full amount. Nahval took my abba before the judges, and they decreed Abba would serve him until the *shmittah*,[17] six full years. Because my uncle was caring for their ima, he was not sold into service, just Abba."

---

16   mother
17   year of release for Hebrew indentured servants

A Hebrew servant. According to the Torah, Avidan's abba would have to sell himself into servitude for up to six years to pay a debt. Tzakhi had heard of Nahval, though, and he was a famously wicked and greedy man like Bilaam. Melekh David planned to kill Nahval, but his wife had secretly entreated Melekh David with gifts to assuage his anger. Not long after, Nahval simply dropped dead, and his wife married Melekh David. It was a romance for the fireside storytellers to sing.

Avidan continued, "Abba simply couldn't serve Nahval. Nahval worked his Hebrew indentured servants until they were cripples, and he treated his slaves worse. So one night, Abba came and took me from my bed. Abba was afraid Nahval would take me in his place if he ran away. Together, we ran."

"To Melekh David?" prompted Tzakhi.

"Yes. Abba heard that Melekh Shaul was hunting David throughout Judea, but David had a little army of his own growing. He was training men to be soldiers, and they were protecting Israelites from bandits and raiding Canaanites. Abba had nothing left to lose but his life, so we sought out David. The Prophet Shmuel had anointed him when he was just a boy. Since all Melekh Shaul's army couldn't kill David, nor could the Philistines or their gigantic soldier, we weren't concerned we were on a fool's mission."

"The lion and bear couldn't, either," added Tzakhi. He'd like to see a bear or a lion. He'd only seen their pelts in the caravan baggage.

"So he said," agreed the captain.

"How old were you?" asked Tzakhi.

"Ten," said Avidan. "With no prospects for inheritance or a trade. Our herd was decimated, and there was no money to apprentice me. Abba said the safest place for a boy like me was in David's army. I could manage the equipment and baggage, and maybe, when David took the throne one day, I could serve in his administration, maybe as a steward."

"But you're a soldier," said Tzakhi. "Not a steward."

"Yes," said Avidan. "As it turned out, everyone in David's camp had to learn the arts of war: sword, spear, archery, sling, hand-to-hand combat, shield, tracking, strategy and tactics, and even diplomacy and reading. I was very good at it. It was easy to learn because I was so young. Because I was surrounded with fighters, the skills came naturally. I've passed all of it on to you. Since you'll know your father's trade, you will always be valuable to kidnappers."

"What happened to your abba?" asked Tzakhi, trying to ignore the last part of Avidan's statement.

"The Amalekites destroyed and plundered our families at the camp in Ziklag while we were off marching with David. They kidnapped our wives and children, including David's wife Avigail, whom he'd married after Nahval died. We pursued the Amalekites across the Negev, defeated them, and retrieved all our property and people along with all the Amalekites' property. Abba's share of the plunder was so much that he had the full amount and much more to pay off the debt to Nahval. He'd never wanted to be on the run. Avigail was grateful to be rescued, and she was more than willing to let Abba redeem the debt without pressing any further charges. Abba went back home and rebuilt the herd."

"And you?"

"I remained with David. When he ruled the first seven years in Chevron, I served, but he could see I was unhappy. He sent me on missions to the south to alleviate my misery because I could not live in a city. I'd grown up in the wilderness, constantly moving, scouting, camping, sleeping under the stars. When he began to build his city in Yerushalayim, he sent me here to manage troops.

I'm old enough now to be content at the fortress, but patrolling with the horse soldiers satisfies my wandering heart. I enjoy training young soldiers the way that Melekh David trained me."

Tzakhi was glad Avidan was stationed here and happy to stay. Conscripted soldiers rarely adjusted, and they were glad when their three-month rotations were up. Avidan had taught Tzakhi sword skills, archery, javelin, spear, and shield work in addition to tracking and riding. He knew as much of weapons as he knew of the desert from the Bedouin boys.

"Life was so much easier when our only real goal was to elude Melekh Shaul," Avidan said. "When David took the throne, the enemy was much harder to know. Even the sons of his own household turned against him. Life was simpler here when we were just do-gooding bandits and mercenary soldiers. The south has always been able to manage itself regardless of who ruled around it. Trade makes friends of enemies. That's why David was able to hide here so long. People mind their own business because that's what it is here in Tamar, business."

Tzakhi had thought to ask Avidan if he had any advice on what to do about the fires, but there would be no point. In Tamar, it was indeed all business. The captain would stay out of Nachshon's plans. He was only there to ensure those plans would be executed.

"You never married?" asked Tzakhi.

The captain looked away, across the desert, as if he could see all the way to the land of two-humped camels and elephants. "Once."

"She died?" asked Tzakhi. Women died a lot. Abba had been married five times. He worried about Shira. She had not yet been found with child, but there were not many skilled midwives in the Arava.

"Yes. I was with Melekh David when he fought Hadadezer, the king of Zobah, as far as Hamat. Melekh David wanted to establish his rule to the Perat River and north into Aram. It was three years before I could return. It was our longest campaign of his reign. When I returned, my wife was dead and my son was gone."

"You had a son, too?" asked Tzakhi.

"Yes. He was very young. He was a son of five years when I left. I was newly stationed here, and it was only a lonely outpost with few people or soldiers. It was mostly a caravansary. I tried to convince my wife to go stay with my family while I was gone, but she was sure I'd be gone only for a summer, our usual battle season. When she died, she had some small debts, which I would have cleared easily when I returned. There was some confusion, and a family paid the debts. They took in my son as surety, then moved on to the Judean hills, and then maybe farther north. When I tried to track them, I lost their movement somewhere around Chevron," said Avidan.

"Where was my abba? He would have helped," said Tzakhi.

"Your abba was working at Timna. He didn't know me well then," said the captain.

"And the family who took him never tried to find you?" asked Tzakhi.

"No. Some people in Chevron remembered a young boy, and some did not remember him at all. I never found him."

Tzakhi asked, "Is that why you always personally inspect the people in the caravans?"

"Yes," said Avidan. "I mention my son's name to see if anyone recognizes it."

"*Tzar*," said Tzakhi.

"*Tzar-li*," replied Avidan with a huskiness in his voice Tzakhi had never heard.

"So now," said Avidan, speeding his gait much faster than one would think of a man in his 50s, "my job is to find out what business our watchers have with the melekh's fortress."

So long ago, so long ago.
The wolves grew gaunt and cubs drowned.
Generations grew dark, yet one was pale.
It was the pack of the earth,
The pack of the sea-wolf.
They fled the fire, they fled the ice.
So long ago, so long ago.

CHAPTER ELEVEN

"Tzakhi."

Tzakhi took up the girth one more notch and buckled it, then he looked over the saddle-cloth at his father, who stood between his two bodyguards. "Yes, Abba?"

"I'll be gone for at least two weeks to Timna. I need to form an extra work crew to harvest acacia wood for the fires after the Feast of Sukkot. I'm sending them farther east where there are more trees. Last winter's floods did not leave so much dried wood behind, and we are struggling for fuel. We are short of charcoal. Help Shira when she asks. Stay close to her in case the bodyguards are needed elsewhere. We are very short-handed."

"Yes, Abba. I will," said Tzakhi.

"That means you need to stay close to the fortress. No wandering in the desert or patrolling with the soldiers. Just work the caravans, load the wood, and take the meals to the givah each day," said Abba. "Stay in the house with Shira at night. Sleep at the door like the shepherds sleep in the gate of the sheepfold."

"Yes, Abba."

Nachshon walked around his sturdy Hittite horse, inspecting Tzakhi's work in bridling and saddling. "You are an expert horseman, Tzakhi. You will miss this when you start working with your brothers. We'll have a few weeks to prepare when I return, and then we'll start the journey to Yerushalayim for Sukkot."

Tzakhi's stomach knotted.

"Yes, Abba."

"Spend some time with The Levite since you need to stay close to the fortress. Learn as much Torah as you can before we leave. You'll be invited to discussions at the Holy Temple and around the holiday meals in Yerushalayim."

Although Tzakhi had memorized long passages from the Torah, he wasn't too sure about discussing it in adult company. Tamar was hardly big enough for any Torah school, and the lone Levite in the fortress was there as a resource for the soldiers and Israelite families. He only had one worn copy of each of the five books of Torah, and the deer hide scrolls had a deep brown patina, making it hard to distinguish the letters.

Tzakhi didn't know why a Levite was willing to spend his life at a desert fortress, but when he'd mentioned it to Avidan one time, Avidan just said, "The Levites have cities of refuge for a man-slayer...but where can a Levite go?"

CHAPTER TWELVE

A shofar rang from the stone walls of the fortress. It was still dark, and Tzakhi heard it from his sleeping mat. It was too early to be the call for the men to say the morning prayer, the *Shema*.

Soldiers. This shofar shout roused soldiers to wake, feed their horses a meal of precious barley grain, and saddle them for a pre-dawn patrol. Then another call sounded. This time, it was the call to muster for a long march. That signaled the stewards to prepare packs of food and skins of water for several days' journey. Where were they going?

In spite of his sleepiness, Tzakhi arose and rolled up the mat and blanket, placing them carefully on a bench to make it harder for scorpions to burrow inside. Slipping into the darkness outside, Tzakhi strained to hear what may have prompted this sudden departure of the soldiers. The guard outside their house looked toward the horse pens where men were starting to move around.

Along with its complement of infantry, one cavalry detachment had left a day earlier to protect the tax money transfer. The other cavalry detachment's departure with its infantry today was to a place yet unknown to Tzakhi. Their absence, however, would empty the fortress of the infantry who guarded the roads and outer gates when not on patrol. Rarely did both detachments vacate the fortress at the same time.

A skeleton foot guard of conscripted soldiers was left. Their company leader was the lone professional. Whatever was pulling the cavalry away must be very important. It left the Tamar fortress vulnerable, especially if the word spread to bandits that the outlying tents of Tamar had few to defend them, much less pursue a fast mounted raid.

The tinkle of bronze buckles, creaking leather, and soldier's grunts filled the morning twilight. "Keep your eyes open, Tzakhi," said Captain Avidan from the darkness.

"Where are you going?" asked Tzakhi.

"A messenger arrived at the gate last night. A very special guest is traveling from Sheba to visit and bring valuable gifts to Melekh Shlomo. We are to meet her caravan coming from Sela and escort her to Ein Gedi. She is bearing young balsam plants to be planted at the gardens there."

"*She?*" asked Tzakhi.

"The Queen of Sheba," said Avidan. "*Malkhat Sheva.*"

Tzakhi didn't know what to say.

"You know the desert better than any of the soldiers left here," said Avidan. "You must be the eyes and ears of the fortress."

"Who is in command while you're gone?" asked Tzakhi.

"Ben-Shimi."

Oh, no. Not the dullest of gatekeepers. And definitely the most gullible.

The lion and the serpent cast the silver bowls,
The copper the gold.
And a golden lion touched a she-wolf
And the silver hair, silver was there.

The lambs lay down in fire,
But the beasts were there
And the silver hair.

CHAPTER THIRTEEN

"Midianite shepherds!" called the tower guard from the south wall.

A few people looked up and southward, but it wasn't a noteworthy approach. The Midianites were coming to water their sheep and probably to trade a little. Tzakhi and The Levite sat in the early morning shade of tamarisk trees adjacent to the well. Baka and Matukah stood under a tree asleep, each with a hind leg bent and propped, totally relaxed. They were waiting for Tzakhi to remove the empty packs from their morning walk up the givah.

A couple of soldiers were watching two scorpions fighting in a wooden box. They were gambling on the outcome with some men from one of the several tent camps around the fortress. When a caravan was at Tamar, the stakes on scorpion-fighting soared, especially when merchants were returning from the seaports with purses full of silver and gold.

The caravansaries were spaced a day's journey apart. Stone pens held scores of camels and donkeys either weak and recovering from a hard journey or well-rested and prepared to be traded to an incoming caravan in exchange for their exhausted camels and silver.

The number of camels in a caravan could number from tens to hundreds. The exchange rate for a fresh camel here in the arid

Arava was much higher than in Egypt or in the north where fresh water, grazing, and fodder were easier to obtain. Merchants and drovers on the trip southward were more willing to part with their coin for a fresh camel than those traveling north to the coast or west to Egypt.

The Levite...few people knew his real name...he was just called The Levite as if no one needed to know his name...motioned to Tzakhi to continue answering his question on the feast of Sukkot. The old scroll of Vayikra[18] lay on a small wooden bench. The Levite had repaired the scroll's deer hide pages many times, binding them back together with fine threads made from dried animal veins, or sometimes scraping a worn letter and re-writing it with a special ink.

Tzakhi bent his head over the scroll, but The Levite reached over and rolled it so Tzakhi could not read. He said, "No, discuss it. Tell about it. You already know what the words say." The Levite threw a piece of worn linen fabric over the scroll to protect it from bird droppings. Sparrows were quick at everything.

Ugh. Tzakhi wasn't much of a talker. There were a lot of words in his head, but one thing he inherited from his abba was the ability to be silent.

"You read the desert sign," suggested The Levite. "This is the same. See, taste, touch, and hear what's beneath the words."

Easy for him to say. The Levite had an assortment of scrolls he'd collected over the years from the caravans. He could read and write much better than Tzakhi. The passage Tzakhi had just read cautioned against idolatry. He knew many of those who camped around the Tamar fortress kept idols in their tents, yet they dared

---

18 Leviticus

not display them openly. Avidan would require the tent be packed and out of sight before the sun set.

"Don't think of what you already know the words say," suggested The Levite. "Think of them literally, as if you barely understood the Hebrew language. As if you were reading something ancient."

It is ancient, thought Tzakhi. *Hundreds of years old.*

"No," said the Levite. "Even older. Without beginning, without end. These are Words of Creation."

How did The Levite know what he was thinking? He gave the man a quizzical look. The Levite smiled and tapped his own head.

Tzakhi tried, "It sounds as if worshiping an idol is putting another god on HaShem's face."

"Excellent!" exclaimed The Levite. "And how do we become idolators?"

"Interest leads to obsession. Obsession leads to idolatry," Tzakhi answered. "Because we desire something, we..." Tzakhi stalled, not sure how to put it.

"It's okay. Think out loud," encouraged The Levite.

"We put our own face on HaShem. Or no, not exactly. We...we take an idol representing what we want. Maybe wealth, or power, or more children. The idol is really us. We put an idol between us and HaShem. Instead of being thankful for HaShem and what He gives us when *He* wants, we prefer to tell the gods and goddesses what *we* want and when we want it. The gods are very much like us because we choose the ones we think will be most like what we want." This sounded very childish to Tzakhi. He always felt childish around The Levite.

"That's quite an insightful explanation, Tzakhi. Remember it when you go to the Temple and discuss the Holy Torah with the scribes. It is something good to contribute." His eyes shined with longing, as if they were Yerushalayim itself. "And remember as much as you can. You must tell me everything when you return."

The tower guard called out again, this time his voice a little more urgent. "Midianites carrying dead or injured!"

A few soldiers hurried to the east gate and retrieved spears, while a few others took archery posts on the south wall. Two other archers joined the spearmen. The fortress was indeed guarded by a tiny squad. Gatekeepers reported to the east gate and stood at the ready to close them.

Curious, Tzakhi and The Levite joined a small group assembling on the hill overlooking the highway from Etzion-Geber and Edom. There was a small flock of sheep, and two shepherds walked behind them leading their donkeys. Across their packs, the donkeys carried a man apiece. From the looks of how their weight had settled, the men were dead or nearly so. The shepherds were both shouldering burdens, probably to make room on the donkeys for the men.

Boys from the outlying tents raced their donkeys toward the fortress, eager to be the first to report the arrival of the disturbing travelers. When they neared the fortress, one shepherd turned the sheep toward the drinking trough, and the other took the lead rope of both donkeys and approached the gate. He was quickly surrounded, for everyone recognized the dead men.

Nachshon's bodyguards.

And yes, dead. Shot through with arrows.

Tzakhi wanted to sink to the ground. He'd never had such an overwhelming feeling of weakness, dizziness almost. Had the desert finally swallowed Abba, too?

The Midianite shepherd dropped his pack and told the story to the growing crowd. Two treasury workers removed the dead soldiers from the donkeys and lowered them gently to the ground.

Because of the arrows, the rigid bodies lay slightly contorted, unable to lay flat.

The shepherd said, "We were moving this herd to sell along the caravansaries," he said. "These soldiers lay in the highway, already dead. We could see horse hoofprints, nothing else. The hoofprints traveled east toward Moab."

Ben-Shimi examined the bodies, looking worried. Tzakhi suspected he wasn't as worried about Nachshon being killed or kidnapped as he was about being held responsible for it. Nachshon wasn't just any man. He was the mind of the king and the defense of the Kingdom when it came to preparing weapons of war.

Tzakhi could see in Ben-Shimi's eyes the fear of a man who didn't know whether his short time feeling the power of authority would cost him the rest of his life. Would Avidan, or worse, Melekh Shlomo, want to know why Ben-Shimi didn't dispatch Shira's bodyguards with Nachshon and guard her door at night himself? Ben-Shimi was probably as scared as Tzakhi, but for a different reason.

It wasn't the first time Tzakhi had seen dead men. It was part of life here. His stomach pitched, however, for he had known the two soldiers. Like Captain Avidan, they weren't reserve troops mustered to serve three months out of the year, but full-time soldiers. Professionals in the king's cavalry.

Next to Avidan, he'd spent more time with the bodyguards than anyone at the fortress. He'd cared for their horses, eaten with them, and even swam with them in the Red Sea. They didn't make fun of his silver hair.

The Levite cut their *tzitziyot*[19] from the hems of their tunics, an act that brought a knot-swallow to Tzakhi's throat. The Levite

---

19 Ritual fringes affixed to the four corners of the garment

never left Tamar, even for the feasts, so he didn't have to maintain the level of ritual purity as other Levites. Unconcerned about touching the dead, The Levite tugged loose the arrows, lay the bodies flat, and arranged their hands and feet. He placed the cut white fringes with their blue cords atop their stomachs. The hands had become too bloated and stiff to move much.

Tzakhi was glad when someone finally placed linen cloths over their faces, but it didn't lessen their stench. Later, each would be wrapped in plain linen and buried in the grave cave to the north of the fortress facing toward Yerushalayim. With the faces covered, it was easier for Tzakhi to disconnect the hideously swollen limbs from the faces of his friends.

The burning question was whether Abba also lay somewhere in the desert bloating in the sun, or whether he was tied to a swift horse on the way northeast to Ashur. From the look on Ben-Shimi's face, the question was burning hot enough to terrify a grown man.

CHAPTER FOURTEEN

"**M**an-stealers?" breathed Tzakhi to Shira's off-duty guard. The guard stood close to Tzakhi as if to protect him from the soldiers' fate.

"Maybe Captain Avidan's detachment will run into them," said the guard. "If the raiders are riding to Ashur." Like Tzakhi, his first thought was meddling by the Ashurim.

"No," said Tzakhi. This guard was fairly new and young, unfamiliar yet with the geography of the South. This was why he was left at the fortress. "The Queen was already at Sela awaiting escort. The raiders would go east and only then north. Unless a messenger rides toward Sela and intercepts the Queen's caravan between there and Ein Gedi, the Captain will not know." He didn't add that the guard should already know that. It went without saying.

The dilemma showed in Ben-Shimi's face. Only a few horses and baggage mules remained at the fortress, and those horses were the ones less swift and strong. With their defense already stretched so far, could they spare a few soldiers for a pursuit?

In the end, Ben-Shimi sent two soldiers on horseback to scout the area of the kidnapping and return with news. He also sent one rider on a fast mule to locate Avidan's detachment. It would be up to Captain Avidan to split his forces into those who would escort the Queen and those who would pursue the man-stealers along the highway through Moab. "By then," said Ben-Shimi, trying to sound confident, "we will have more information from the scouts, and we can send a rider with the scouting report to the captain."

It wasn't a bad plan. It wasn't a good one, either. It gave the man-stealers at least three days' head start in addition to the two days the Midianites had taken to walk to Tamar. After that, how many days would Avidan need to search for a small raiding party?

Shira took it harder than Tzakhi would have expected. Abba was never demonstrative with Shira around Tzakhi. If they wanted to be alone, Abba simply told Tzakhi to go check on the donkeys. There was no need to tell Tzakhi that...he cared for them diligently...so it was just understood that Tzakhi needed to leave the house for an hour or so. Whatever affection they might have for one another must have been saved for those alone times.

Although Shira didn't cry, she alternately spoke kindly and snapped at him. It was probably frustrating not to be able to just walk through Tamar and talk to anyone you wanted when you needed information. The next day, she pestered him until he let her sit with him on the fortress wall to watch for riders, and it gave her bodyguard a break as well.

Tzakhi sat atop the fortress wall, watching a donkey caravan approach from the south, each donkey laden with a pack of dried fish from the Red Sea. The last of a camel caravan disappeared west into the tawny open jaws of the mountains. The spice trail was dangerous. Flash floods, loose rocks, sheer cliffs, robbers, relentless heat, scorpions, and vipers. Man-stealers.

Why did the caravans continue, one after the other, year after year? What pushed them along on blistered feet, over camel-dung pavers, absorbing the stink of donkeys and unwashed human bodies? What made the spices they carried so treasured that buyers paid a man enough to risk his life, exchanging light pouches of dried plants for heavy ones of gold? What were light and heavy, really? And who decided the value of spices or a man's life? Tzakhi posed those questions to Shira, but she wasn't really listening. She was looking.

Shira already thought him a strange boy, but she didn't mind it. She said in the Palace of Women, there weren't many men around, so all men were strange to her. Tzakhi's dreamy musings weren't getting her attention, so he tried a different tack to keep her mind off what had happened to Abba.

"How did you learn how to make the unguents?" Tzakhi asked her.

"From the compounders who prepared cosmetics for the Palace of Women. Sometimes they let me help. They let me ask questions about what aromas went together and what didn't. People smell things differently, so much of the art was knowing what the women liked and what the melekh liked on the women."

That silenced Tzakhi. Every boy in Israel wondered about the Palace of Women, but it wasn't proper to talk about with his stepmother. Shira probably said it precisely to silence him. He didn't usually talk this much, so she knew what he was doing.

As if she understood, Shira said softly, "It's okay, Tzakhi. You don't have to cheer me up. I'll be okay."

Tzakhi knew he should spend more time comforting Shira, but on the second day, he had to leave her at the house. He had to haul fodder for the donkeys and send up some extra supplies to the givah.

When he finished, she had some food packed for them, and she accompanied him back to the southern wall. They anxiously watched the road from Paran. The tower guard was sympathetic, and thankfully, he was appeased with a warm roll of flatbread, goat cheese, walnuts, and dates. He didn't try to make small talk, and he even insisted Shira sit under the tower's shade cloth.

They stayed atop the wall until evening, when Shira's bodyguards returned to walk her home. They had become even more attentive, so Tzakhi didn't worry about her safety.

At home, she cried a little, but not too much, then after supper, she busied herself with compounding balms for Tzakhi to sell to the caravans. She was smarter than he, keeping herself busy and distracted rather than feel the slow crawl of seconds, minutes, and hours.

When the scouts returned that night, Tzakhi heard the shofar. He and Shira walked to the little hill near the well and waited to hear news from the incoming riders.

The information was puzzling. "As many as twenty-five or thirty horses," said the one with a little more experience. "The winds had already erased many of the tracks. The strange thing is it doesn't look like that many horses traveled east."

"Where did the other tracks lead?" asked Ben-Shimi.

"Maybe...maybe...west," said the scout. "It was much harder to pick up sign, almost as if they concealed the tracks by dragging something behind them. Even so, we found the odd hoofprint. No droppings, though. If some of them went west, they were much more careful. I think they took Nachshon east, and maybe the tracks going west were mercenaries who assisted with the kidnaping, but they were paid and are returning to their tents. Amalekite Bedouin, maybe, or Ishmaelite traders. Ishmaelites are excellent archers. The arrows were placed so precisely into our men that I think it's the best explanation."

"You think Ishmaelites or Amalekites?" asked Ben-Shimi.

"Yes, it is the only explanation I can think of. Either would know not to associate themselves with kidnaping Melekh Shlomo's chief metalworker. They'd want to part ways as soon as possible and create distance," said the scout.

Ben-Shimi, rather than being insulted that the scout didn't relay the information and leave it to him to draw the conclusions, seemed relieved. If the scout were wrong, then it might deflect some responsibility from him for making a poor choice in what to do next.

"Ben-Shimi," said Tzakhi. "Let me go to Timna to inform my oldest brother Elad. I need to warn him and my other brothers. Elad is Abba's second-in-command. He will know what to do."

The hesitancy of a few minutes before was replaced by irritation. Ben-Shimi lifted his chin smugly at Tzakhi. "You're just a boy. I'm not going to risk you wandering off the highway to hunt for lizards, or worse yet, lose you to bandits as well. Did you think I hadn't already hired a messenger to send for Elad? Someone has to supervise the furnace."

Everyone looked at Tzakhi. No one would talk to Tzakhi like that if his abba were there unless it was a caravan drover who didn't know him. Even then, Tzakhi didn't mind. It made him feel normal, not a son and brother of fire-men. Now, though, the scorn was intentional. A declaration of superiority, like a rank donkey harassing the others in a pen. Maybe if Ben Shammai were about to be blamed for losing Nachshon, he was going to leave a few heart-felt words.

Ben-Shimi added, "And don't try to sneak off. I'm going to have the gate-soldiers watch to make sure you stay at the fortress. You go no further than Givat Chatzeva."

What Ben-Shimi did next was exactly what he'd said he'd do. With the last fresh horse, he remounted the more experienced scout and dispatched him to find Captain Avidan.

CHAPTER FIFTEEN

The longer Tzakhi stood there, the more it didn't add up.
No.

No.

The Ishmaelite and Amalekite Bedouin knew better than to take that kind of mercenary job. Melekh Shlomo might not dispatch an army to recover some lost goods or donkeys from a robber raid, but once he heard about the loss of his chief metalworker, he'd march half his army and put to death anyone who might have had something to do with it.

The melekh had placed fifty fortresses in the Arava and Negev precisely to drive out the raiding Amalekites. They didn't want more pressure, for there was nowhere to go except into neighboring nations who didn't want them. If it were Amalekites, it would have to be the most renegade of renegades. Worst of the worst.

The Ishmaelites had been on friendly terms since the reign of Melekh David.

No.

If some of the horses went west, and the riders had taken pains to conceal it, it wasn't normal mercenary Bedouin. Only an expert tracker would be able to read it. Abba must have been carried west somewhere in the vast wilderness. Tzakhi was likely the only person left in all of Tamar who could find him. He turned quickly and walked toward his house.

She knew when he walked through the door. "You can't," Shira said, rising from her little wooden worktable. "Whatever it is, no, please. I see it in your eyes."

"I have to, Shira," said Tzakhi. "They're looking in the wrong direction. The only soldiers still here don't know how to track or survive. The other men who live here and could pursue, won't. A band of raiders big and powerful enough to steal the king's chief mine steward is nothing the men here would risk pursuing without a detachment of soldiers."

"So what could *you* do?" asked Shira. "Just watch?"

"Exactly," said Tzakhi. "I can track them. If I'm wrong, then I just come back home. Nothing is different. If I find them, then I can send a carrier dove or Baka home with a note telling where they are or where I think they are going. All I have to do is track and watch until Captain Avidan can catch up. Or I can notify the closest outpost, and they will send soldiers. Don't worry."

Shira, of course, objected to his plan, but even as she argued, she prepared him a full pack of flatbreads, dates, raisin cakes, fig cakes, nuts, roasted barley, dried porgy and gazelle meat, a flask of olive oil, and his night cloak. "I'll lose you both," she said. "You're my only real friend, Tzakhi, and the wilderness will take you both. The desert swallows weak and strong alike here. It loves no one."

"I'll be careful, Shira," said Tzakhi. "And listen closely. If I find Abba, I'll send Baka or Matukah back with a message tied into the mane. It will tell where he is. I can just watch until the captain and cavalry arrive. If they move, I'll follow the trail and leave sign."

"A lone donkey walking in the Arava?" said Shira doubtfully. "The wolves and jackals will kill her." Some tears shined in her eyes, but Shira didn't sob. As much as Tzakhi worried Shira had given up on life, he didn't want to be the one who made her give up completely. He felt a pang of guilt. If she were a man, he knew she'd go, too.

"Pray to HaShem, Shira," said Tzakhi. "And if something happens to Abba and me, then you can return to your father's house. Life will be easier for you."

"Who would pay such a price for comforts, Tzakhi?"

"Promise me you won't give up, Shira. If your father will permit it, sell your jewelry and balms. Make a place for yourself. A government official in one of the caravans said that there is a noblewoman in Yerushalayim who is an official of the king. She is an administrator, and she even has her own signet ring. Find her, and maybe she can help, yes?" asked Tzakhi.

Shira said, "With such reasoning, you should let your abba be carried away so you will not have to serve the fires."

That stopped Tzakhi short, and the momentary confusion must have shown on his face.

"Stay or go, Tzakhi. I will begin praying the tehillim of *saba* Melekh David. She held out a small package wrapped in folded doeskin, tied in a scarlet thread. Here. I made this as a gift for you to take to Yerushalayim at Sukkot, but maybe you should have it now."

Tzakhi opened the layers of the leather folds carefully, like he'd remove petals from a winter crocus to find the precious stem within. Inside was a small copper scroll amulet resting in a soft leather pouch with a thong necklace. Shira said, "It's rolled inside, but the letters say, '*Zev tzach*.' Something to remember your mother and her tribe always." *Dazzling wolf.* Bright, like the sun shining on the desert.

Tzakhi hugged Shira and kissed both her cheeks gratefully. "If my ima had a daughter, Shira, she'd want her to be just like you. Me, too. You're the sister I would want. Thank you."

"And here..." Shira handed him two knitted objects made of different colors of yarn. "I used some scraps of yarn to make new fly bonnets for your donkeys like the Bedouin. They're not very good, but I'm learning to knit and weave from the tax administrator's servant."

"This is very kind, Shira. Thank you again," said Tzakhi. He would have liked one for himself. The desert flies of late summer were a swarming plague. When they were especially bad, all he could do was cover the lower part of his face by wrapping the end of his turban from ear to ear. In high summer, sometimes he dipped the turban in Shira's lavender-and-mint oil, which helped repel insects.

"If you find your abba, tell him I'll have the olive relish prepared that he loves so much. And promise me you'll be careful, Tzakhi."

"I promise."

Feeling bad that Shira was so helpless, but resolved to find Abba, Tzakhi walked to the stable to prepare Baka and Matukah. He kept an eye open for soldiers who might be watching his movements, but the thin force was spread around the gates and towers. As Tzakhi settled a pack on Baka's back, he felt a presence approach the shed.

It was The Levite. With a long knife.

CHAPTER SIXTEEN

The Levite unbuckled his belt. Rolling the belt so the long, two-edged iron knife lay atop in its leather scabbard, he handed it to Tzakhi. "Your flint knife is fine for honest work, but not for defending yourself. Be careful."

Tzakhi took it and assessed its weight. It was very similar to Avidan's spare short sword, with which he'd practiced many times, but only with an acacia wood frame fitted around the blade to prevent injuries.

The Levite said, "You saw Ben-Shimi look toward the place of the Edomite's tent when he recognized the dead. Ben-Shimi probably spoke of Nachshon's plans to the Edomite or one of his... slaves. The Edomite trades in all sorts of things, including pleasure for information, so he knows the coming and going of the administrators and soldiers. When he moves his tent to Botzrah, Sela, and the other caravansaries, the Edomite is acquiring information, not just fresh customers. He pulled up his tent and left the morning before your abba's journey, which might have been a signal to someone watching that the time was right to take Nachshon."

"How does that help find Abba?" asked Tzakhi.

"It helps to know who might be involved. The Edomite may be just an evil trader of human beings and pleasures, but he may be involved in something much bigger. You know Melekh David nearly wiped out the Edomite army?"

"*Ken*," said Tzakhi. "Avidan told me about it. He's never liked the Edomite hanging around. Says he was too cowardly to fight with his people."

"The Edomite survivors of the battles...including their prince Hadad...fled to Egypt. There Pharaoh protected them and raised the lad Sar Hadad like a son. He wanted to adopt him, even gave him his own sister for a wife. Melekh Shlomo's advisors tried to persuade him to talk to Pharaoh about banishing Sar Hadad or sending him back to Israel to be imprisoned, but the king rejected the advice. Pharaoh put Sar Hadad in charge of many of his trade alliances."

"That is an uneasy situation," said Tzakhi, who knew when a deal was impossible to make.

The Levite continued, "Yes, and more uneasy because Melekh Shlomo's Egyptian wife knew Hadad as a brother, and she interceded for his protection.[20] Since then, we have heard rumblings that Sar Hadad and his son Genuvat have been making alliances, trying to prepare the way for his return to Edom to regain control of his inheritance. The copper mines made them rich, especially when they formed partnerships with Egypt. Now Melekh Shlomo is becoming rich from the mines they consider theirs."

"How could he do that?" asked Tzakhi. "The Pharaoh would not sabotage Melekh Shlomo. He would not give Hadad weapons or an army."

The Levite answered, "The sons of Nevaiot from Botzra have aligned themselves with Sar Hadad to lengthen their trade routes as far as Tarshish. They want to compete with Tyre and Sidon.

---

20   1 Kings 11

Melekh Shlomo tolerates the trade competition because his ships are already loaded with goods. He settles for the taxes he collects from them when they pass through his collection points. Young Genuvat has spent much time with the Kittim and their warriors. Sar Hadad and Genuvat are coordinating trade to raise an army."

"How do you know all this?" asked Tzakhi.

"Do you think with hundreds of wives and concubines that the walls do not hear and tell?"

Tzakhi shrugged. Shira wasn't a gossip, but men seemed to think all women did. It was hypocritical because all men did was gossip and tell lies around the caravan fires and guard towers at night. Sheep-shearing times were the worst because the celebration wine loosened their tongues. Since most women were excluded from public life, maybe that was how they found out what was going on in the world.

Tzakhi asked, "But what does that have to do with Abba? Sar Hadad is more Egyptian than Edomite. Pharaoh already has craftsmen who know almost as much as what Abba knows. Sar Hadad doesn't need to kidnap Melekh Shlomo's."

"True," said The Levite. "But Sar Hadad's influence has spread to other countries. The rumor of his desire to return to Edom is a clever bit of misdirection. His son Genuvat has been sailing often across the Great Sea[21] to Latium,[22] a country of the Kittim near Yavan.[23] It is rather primitive and barbaric, but the Kitti warriors are said to be brutal and strong. The prince has been going there under the guise of establishing trade for Pharaoh along the Tiber River, but the rumors are that he is actually trying to establish a kingdom there. Trade is important, but if he can influence the

---

21   Mediterranean
22   Italy
23   Greece

military men, he can take power, perhaps reign there as a vassal state of Egypt. He's married one of their women."

"And how does it help Sar Hadad and his son to establish a kingdom so far away if they want to re-take Edom?" asked Tzakhi.

The Levite said, "Edom's army was destroyed by Melekh David, so it is likely he is trying to raise an army to return here and seize Edom from Israel. He needs an expert metalworker with the secrets of bronze and iron to equip a large number of men who can fill the trade ships he's building. Genuvat could control trade with his army on the Great Sea, and Sar Hadad could control the land routes between Edom and Tyre. It's a pincer strategy."

"Why don't they simply raise production of their bronze weapons?" asked Tzakhi. "Not all Israelite soldiers carry iron weapons. Some of the bronze is still better than iron."

"Because," said The Levite. "Egypt is now producing inferior bronze and iron to your abba. Nachshon and Melekh Shlomo collaborated on secret alloys with the Tyrian craftsman. Melekh Shlomo spent much time with Khiram, whose father was a master metalworker in Tyre. He's the son of an Israelite mother from Naphtali, though, so he's been very generous with his knowledge. Melekh Shlomo has the Tyrian ships bring the special tin for bronze from farther away than any other kingdom has before. Your father has been experimenting with the iron up on Givat Chatzeva. The secrets are perhaps the only thing Melekh Shlomo has not shared with his Egyptian woman."

Tzakhi sensed some bitterness in The Levite's words. The only person who could have known such a detail about the improved quality of the bronze or smelting iron was Abba or one of Tzakhi's older half-brothers.

Did Abba trust The Levite that much? It might explain why Abba was always sending Tzakhi to learn with him when he noticed him with a little free time. It was still too fantastic to believe completely. Maybe The Levite was involved and trying to misdirect him. "Melekh Shlomo is too powerful for Sar Hadad to defeat," Tzakhi objected.

"His Egyptian wife has introduced her idols into the high places already," said The Levite. "It is only a matter of time until idolatry seeps into the Yerushalayim palace itself. Melekh Shlomo and his sons will fall from power when that happens. It is like Shimshon's[24] long hair. Once the hair of the *nazir* was cut because of Delilah, he lost his strength. It is the same with idols. Avidan knows this, which is why he smashes any idols he sees in the camps around the fortress."

Tzakhi tried to process what The Levite was saying. He finally took a long look at the man's face, something disrespectful for someone his age to do to a man that age, but that was the thing. How old was The Levite? Forty years old? Fifty? Younger? In its dry climate, the desert winds carved deep wadis across a person's face.

As if understanding his need to see him as more than a Torah tutor, The Levite said, "Tamar is my prison, Tzakhi, so I collect information about the places I will never go again. Unlike the Edomite and the sons of Nevaiot, though, I don't trade human souls. I teach a bit of Torah to Israelite travelers, pray blessings, scribe, buy blue dye and sell *techelet*,[25] kosher slaughter, and help the physician."

Tzakhi absorbed the conversation, mentally overlaying it with what he understood so far of the man-stealers' tactics. Did he trust The Levite?

"I need some scraps of parchment," said Tzakhi.

---

24 Samson
25 Purplish-blue dye made from the excretion of a sea snail, the *chilazon*.

"I'll bring it to you with a bit of ink and a feather."

"I also need someone to distract the guard on the western tower tonight," added Tzakhi.

"I'll go there and do some late-evening teaching at the second watch. The guard will be glad for the company."

"You killed someone?" asked Tzakhi, still not fully trusting The Levite's cooperation. He'd always been just a man who was over-educated for a desert caravansary. Out of place. "Why?"

The Levite patted the leather scabbard. "You can't ask a Levite to sit by while his sister is violated. But such a story is for a sleepless night. You have things to do. I will pray for your journey." He placed his hands firmly atop Tzakhi's head, bowed his own head slightly, and recited from the Torah:

> *He led you through the great and terrible wilderness,*
> *With its fiery serpents and scorpions*
> *And thirsty ground where there was no water;*
> *He brought water for you out of the rock of flint.*[26]

"Amein," said Tzakhi, rotely responding to the holy words, but uneasy.

The Levite added, "May HaShem send the *tzirah* before you."

---

26 Deuteronomy 8:15

CHAPTER SEVENTEEN

Tzakhi was not so sure that the tzirah, a ghostly, fiery serpent-scorpion could be depended upon to help, but he collected things that might prove useful. Being an expert packer helped him to assemble the bundles for Baka to carry easily. Not everyone was good at it because a person had to think ahead and measure the weight of the object against the need for it to be accessed quickly or packed and unpacked daily. Fragility mattered, too.

Ben-Shimi would probably have someone watching him, so he'd be unable to take a rock dove from the dovecote. He'd have to pack inside the donkey shelter as if he were preparing Baka and Matukah for a trip up to the furnace. He packed a kit of:

A pair of Abba's old sandals and an extra pair of his own
Scraps of oiled leather
A pouch of parchments and a wax-sealed small pot of ink
A hoof cleaning and trimming tool
Ten omers of cracked barley
Extra palm-fiber rope and leather thongs
Several small, lidded, tightly-woven baskets, each with a fighting scorpion
An extra shallow jar for watering the donkeys

A rough cloth for a shade and camouflage
Shira's jar of lavender and mint oil fly repellent
A cloth bag of the yellow dust
Several wax-sealed small trading jars of Shira's fragrant ointments
A night cloak and blanket
A small hollow reed and bow drill for starting fires

To these things he added the dried scapula bone of a young ox, placing it vertically in the corner of the packsaddle so the flared end didn't take up room in the pack. Full extra water-skins he secured across Baka's shoulders like saddlebags.

Matukah was too young to carry real weight, so Tzakhi put the light reed basket pack on her. All she would carry was the foodstuffs Shira prepared and an extra pair of waterskins.

When the sun fully set, Tzakhi hung the shofar, flint knife, bow, and quiver across his shoulders by their straps. He concealed the leather belt under his cloak, took up his walking staff, and led his donkeys to the western outer gate. If he heard nothing in the next few minutes, he'd know The Levite had distracted the guard long enough. He and the girls needed about ten minutes to become indistinguishable among the sand hills and black goat hair tents.

Tzakhi could not believe Abba was stolen by the Ashurim. The search party probably was searching in exactly the wrong direction. If Abba was being taken to the Great Sea, that presented a whole new set of questions.

The Egyptian and Israelite outposts would notice a captive if the man-stealers stopped at the caravansaries or fortresses. There were over fifty small fortresses dotting the Negev highlands from Makhtesh Ramon, a great crater of beautiful sands and seashells, and Kadesh-Barnea on the road to Egypt. The hilltop fortresses kept the nomadic and deadly Amalekites from disrupting the caravan trade routes.

The administrators captured the sparse rain when it filled the wadis, and then stored the water in broad cisterns to farm a little and for drinking water. The small fortresses were not built along roads, but on hilltops for a view of the next fortress and to see any smoke signals. The walls of the fortress were simply shaped to fit the shape of the hilltop.

Friendlier nomads camped around the fortresses, benefiting from the military security and trading. Already the word of Nachshon's kidnaping would have traveled to the Great Sea by those hilltop signals, carrier doves, and travelers. The news would travel faster than horses and camels. Many eyes would be watching, looking for an opportunity to rescue Melekh Shlomo's charash and reap a treasure in reward.

The man-stealers would need to disappear into the desert to wait for the searchers to commit several days in the wrong direction. After that, they'd need a route to a seaport that avoided prying eyes. Ashdod or Ashkelon, maybe?

They'd need to know exactly the route through the Arava and Negev in order to water themselves and their horses, perhaps splitting into three detachments, one as an advance party for each leg of the journey. A night arrival with their captive about twenty bowshots from a fortress or caravansary could be met with fresh riders, horses, food, and water. They could keep Abba shielded from prying eyes for nearly the entire journey.

This was how some merchants avoided the tax station at Tamar, bypassing it, working in two groups to resupply water by leapfrogging camps. Melekh Shlomo's tax collectors solved that by building an additional tax booth at the entrance to the Scorpion's Ascent, a bottleneck impossible to avoid by watering at Ein Tzin.

If the wolves and scorpions didn't attack at night in the Tzin wadi, then the tax collectors would certainly bite them before they began the hot, thirsty ascent to Judah. One could die from thirst much more quickly in the Arava, sometimes mere hours after the threshold of dehydration was crossed.

Yes, the desert itself was the man-stealers' worst enemy, as dangerous to Abba as the swords and arrows they carried. A plan to secure water was only as good as the perfect execution of the plan. What if something impaired their escape? What if they lacked desert craft? Many bones were found in the wilderness, some not far from a source of water. The desert amplified tiny mistakes into fatal ones. If the man-stealers weren't very skilled, Abba wouldn't die by the sword, but thirst.

Tzakhi looked south and west. He knew a place. If he was right, their choice of a hideout was tactically brilliant and audacious. It was there he would go.

CHAPTER EIGHTEEN

As he walked between the donkeys, Tzakhi thought of the Scorpions' Ascent falling away behind him. The *Ma'ale Akkrabim*. Its twisted path up and down the mountains was like a scorpion's tail, yet the legend of the tzirah also hovered there. Eventually, if the man-stealers were aiming for the seaport of Ashkelon, they'd need to cross it.

There were simply too many people and outposts if they traveled to Gaza. If Sar Hadad was responsible for the raid, it wasn't likely with the full knowledge of Pharaoh. They'd want to avoid Egyptian eyes or those who would notify Melekh Shlomo's soldiers and administrators in return for a rich reward from a grateful king.

It was impossible for caravans to elude the small tax collection outpost on the approach to the Akkrabim, but with a small band of riders, it was possible. One only needed a distraction for the guards, and a few horses with leather tied around their hooves could slip quietly up the trail at night.

The Scorpions' Ascent was more like a viper. It was a stepped serpentine path leading from the arid Arava wilderness to the Judean hills. The steep Akkrabim ascent was accomplished through a series of switchbacks, but even then, it wasn't a route to be climbed in the demonic heat of a summer day. Maybe in winter, but definitely not in the late summer. It was a route to be ascended exactly like a serpent, slow and winding in the shadows of evening or morning.

Scorpions weren't killers like vipers, though. A scorpion was a tormentor. The sting from its curled tail was agony. The ancients believed there was a scorpion unlike those of the wilderness. This scorpion, the *tzirah*, could fly like a locust or hornet. It came from the depths of the earth, from Sheol, and its favorite target was the Egyptians, sometimes the Canaanites. The ancient Israelite leaders, Moshe and Yehoshua, could command the army of tzirah. The tzirah attacked first "above," by blinding and confusing its victim. Once the victim was disoriented, it struck below so he could no longer father children.

Flying scorpions. Serpents. Wolves. Donkeys. Fast Egyptian horses. If only Abba's life wasn't at stake, what an interesting story this would make around the caravan fires at night.

CHAPTER NINETEEN

Together Tzakhi and the donkeys walked the wilderness path. The man-stealers weren't stupid. They'd made some clever moves. Sending a few horsemen toward Moab for the soldiers to pursue was smart. But lingering with an Egyptian horse so close to the fortress before the raid was sloppy. Failing to conceal horse droppings was very sloppy.

Any fourteen-year-old could tell the difference between donkey and horse droppings, and horseback riders were rare in the desert. Only royalty, the wealthy, and military could afford swift horses here. Camels and donkeys were much better suited to survive the scarcity of good fodder and water. It took great wealth to sustain horses and their finicky stomachs.

On the other hand, maybe the man-stealers were relying on the speed of their escape to negate the advantage of reading their trail signs. They were convinced of the success of their ruse. Or maybe like The Levite said, they knew in advance that the soldiers would be busy elsewhere.

If Tzakhi were right about their location, it would take three days of walking at night and the cool hours of the day to reach them. He couldn't travel the main highway to Timna and Etzion-Geber because it would be impossible to intercept them. If he stopped to hunt or had to circumvent human or mountain obstacles and impassable canyons, maybe it would take longer than three days.

By taking this route, he was gambling everything. If he were right, he'd either reach their camp without observation, or he'd meet them traveling back toward the Scorpions' Ascent. If he were wrong, he was in for a long, hot, empty journey.

As Tamar fell behind them, Tzakhi's band of three traversed the soft sand waves, rock fields, peeling earth, and hard sand-crust ledges cut by winter flash floods. Their feet and hooves logged the ever-cycling sounds of progress: silence, crunching, rasping, scraping, silence, crunching, rasping, scraping...

It was in the first day's camp that he realized they were more than a pack of three. The wolfpack was following them. A semi-circle of watchers appeared around the camp, hemming Tzakhi and the donkeys into the side of a small givah with a sheer wall. Tzakhi had chosen it to shade them from the sun and anyone who might be watching from the south.

After that, the wolves trailed them, sometimes disappearing for a few hours, sometimes following closely. Always silently. Baka didn't like them following too closely, and she'd switch her tail in irritation. Matukah didn't seem to mind. Maybe being younger, she was enjoying the new view instead of the daily trail to the givah. Tzakhi knew the gait of a predator in the desert. Wolves gave no indication when they were following for a meal. They just trotted behind patiently until a target presented itself as a lagger or wanderer. It was then they leapt into their deadly formation.

Tzakhi wasn't sure why they followed. He was sure, however, that the tawny she-wolf was communicating something to him. When he stopped to rest, and the pack was close, the Mother Wolf stared at him and panted lightly, ignoring the inquisitive sniffs and nudges of her family.

It wasn't the thought of a sane person, but Tzakhi wondered if he and Salmah were somehow connected with wolves more than other animals. The Tribe of Benjamin's standard and their ancient blessing was the wolf:

Benjamin is a ravenous wolf;
In the morning he devours the prey,
And in the evening he divides the spoil.[27]

Although the father's tribe determined the childrens', which made Tzakhi Jewish under the standard of the lion, he and Salmah looked nothing like abba. Why else would these desert predators, only below leopards and caracals on the Arava food chain, allow him and Salmah so close without harm?

It was said that Melekh Shlomo spoke the language of animals, which Tzakhi only partially believed. They said the king spoke intelligently of trees, from the cedar that is in Lebanon even to the hyssop growing on the wall; he spoke also of animals and birds and reptiles and fish. When Tzakhi asked Shira about it, she smiled and said yes, she heard that, too, and her father did have a menagerie of exotic animals, but she'd never seen him talk to them.

Of course, she'd rarely spoken to her father. The king's palace was called The House of the Forest of Lebanon, and it was separate from the palaces of the lesser wives and concubines.

Tzakhi knew animals had their own ways of communicating, and maybe he believed Adam and Chavah[28] could talk to animals in Gan Eden,[29] but could people really do it now? The Levite said

---

27   Genesis 49:27
28   Eve
29   Garden of Eden

Moshe and Yehoshua could control the supernatural, fiery tzirah. Some travelers told stories of wild animals who helped humans, like the dolphins in the Red Sea that had protected overboard sailors from sharks, but those stories, too, smelled a little fantastic, a little too embellished.

Still, here they were. Maybe like jackals, the wolves were trailing a hunter to feed on what was left of a carcass. Or they knew one boy leading two donkeys in this howling wilderness was likely to make a fatal mistake. Maybe the pack would turn back when Tzakhi left their hunting grounds. Maybe they were just curious.

CHAPTER TWENTY

But the wolves didn't turn back.

The second day, he set up a shade under an acacia tree so he and the donkeys could sleep during the day's heat. Only a short series of fitful naps was possible in the blistering temperature. That evening, Tzakhi took his bow and quiver, walked a distance from the camp, and scanned the horizon.

He chose a small rise topped by broken rock, maybe a place where long ago fish once swam in and out of its protective spaces. Abba said the desert used to be a sea. Its salty sand and rock still held seashells and snail shells from an ancient time.

It didn't take long. As Tzakhi sat still, bow strung across his knee, a large hare emerged from a clump of dried weeds. It hopped several amot away and began feeding in another clump.

Wolves hunted by working angles. While a few of the faster wolves chased a hare, the slower ones took wider paths on either side of the hare, not allowing it to turn into cover or lose the pursuers by rapidly changing the angles. Tzakhi had a less stressful demise in mind for this hare.

Another hare took a few hops out of the same clump. Tzakhi silently raised his bow and shot the larger hare. The shot was clean, and the hare didn't cry out, which made Tzakhi glad. It didn't spook the second hare, nor did he want the animal to suffer.

The second hare stood up tall, watching the first hare where it lay. When the first hare didn't move, the second one took a few more hops, moving its long ears this way and that. Tzakhi waited to re-fit the bowstring until its head turned completely, then waited motionless again while the second hare scanned again. One more head-turn. Be patient.

And then the hare returned to all fours and turned away, sniffing something on the ground. Tzakhi sent his second arrow away quickly, severing the hare's spinal cord at the neck. It, too, fell instantly without crying out. Avidan had drilled him endlessly on precision shots, and it paid off. Tzakhi collected the hares and walked back to the camp.

After carefully extracting his arrows and checking to see if the valuable iron arrowheads were still seated properly, he returned them to his quiver. The Arava wolves were night hunters, but if they were following him all night, Tzakhi didn't know if they were eating.

Just in case they were waiting for him and the donkeys to be the main course of a big feast, he wanted to offer them the hares. These weren't normal wolves...well, they were definitely normal wolves, but they weren't behaving normally. They'd left their own hunting grounds.

Tzakhi didn't want to blow his shofar because he didn't want human ears to hear it, but he could perfectly imitate a wolf howl. He blew once and listened, but there was no answer. Once again he blew, and then he walked the length of two bowshots from the camp toward a little clump of dead acacias. He'd guessed right. The wolves had napped there while he and the donkeys slept through the hot part of the day. They were already sitting up, alerted either by the shofar or his scent long before he arrived.

The tawny mother wolf trotted forward, sat, and yawned.

"Shalom," said Tzakhi.

The she-wolf panted slowly in answer, revealing a bright pink tongue and perfect long, white teeth.

Tzakhi threw one hare, and then the other between them. The other wolves didn't move from their places, but they stirred, some standing, others ducking heads low, ears stiff, all eyes locked onto the meal-gift. "A covenant," said Tzakhi to the she-wolf. "We will watch for one another. *Mitzpeh*. If this is what you're doing by following me, then I agree."

The mother-wolf gave a wolf-smile, walked forward, and selected one of the hares. The bigger wolves bounded forward and shared the other one while the younger two waited to see if the Mother Wolf would leave enough for them to also feed. When the pack had devoured the meat and crunched the bones, they rolled in the carcasses, concealing their predator smell.

As Tzakhi walked back to his camp, he felt better about what the wolves might be doing. He'd offered himself alone, and they didn't bite.

Donkeys were vicious defenders, often kept among sheep to help defend against predators. They could kick and bite rapidly, killing and maiming. The wolves would be careful about approaching as long as Baka was close. But Tzakhi had tested the she-wolf, giving her the opportunity to make him a risk-free meal that would last her pack for a few days. He'd never once felt danger.

The Levite had blessed him with the protection of the tzirah to go ahead of him, a creature Tzakhi wasn't sure even existed, but he could clearly see the wolfpack behind him. Maybe it was the copper scroll Shira had given him, but surely not. That would be some kind of sorcery, prohibited by the Holy Torah.

Sometimes there were shadows around him when there were no clouds above. They moved like birds, but then they were gone.

Was this the tzirah or his imagination? Maybe The Levite just planted strange thoughts in his mind.

At camp, Tzakhi pulled his cloak over his head to pray and recited the Shema.

When he finished, he gathered the donkeys, and they walked on in the darkness.

So long ago, so long ago.
The creatures left Egypt,
Creatures of earth,
Creatures of sea.
The water was bitter,
The water was vile.
Then a sea of crystal surrounded them,
A sea of bread, a rock of the sea.

CHAPTER TWENTY-ONE

The next day, Tzakhi shot a huge porcupine and a few chukar at a spring. After skinning the porcupine of its hide, he carefully plucked the quills and bound them together with a leather thong. The tawny wolf was a little more cautious about the meal, first sniffing it thoroughly, then she took a portion and left the rest to the pack.

While Baka and Matukah munched a bit of cracked barley, Tzakhi field-dressed and roasted the chukar over a small acacia fire. The bird's entrails he threw to the pack, who devoured that as well. They'd started sleeping closer to the camp, something Baka still wasn't happy about. A gazelle would have satisfied both Tzakhi and the pack, but it would take days to locate a foraging trail and to lie in wait unless he encountered a bedouin kite.

A kite was made of two stone, parallel walls that narrowed, converging at a drop from a cliff. The Bedouin would surprise the gazelles, frightening them to run through the kite until they ran over the cliff. Afterward, they'd harvest the carcasses. No Israelite could use a kite, for the Torah forbade eating animals killed in such an inhumane way.

Nevertheless, a kite would indicate a known foraging route where Tzakhi could conceal himself and take a gazelle with his bow. This would take too much time, though. He'd have to camp the donkeys downwind a few thousand amot away to prevent the gazelles from picking up human scent.

No, he'd hunt hares and rodents for the wolves, but he'd need to sustain himself with the food he'd brought and hope to sight more partridge or chukar. If he couldn't find Abba at Har Karkom, he'd have to stick carefully to the trails between the sparse springs and hunt to survive the trip back to Tamar or seek out his brothers in Timna.

The third day, early fall clouds hung low over the desert. This was as dangerous as night predators and merciless heat. If it were raining even far away, flash floods could fill a wadi and overtake an unwitting traveler. And two donkeys. The wolfpack wasn't in sight.

Taking advantage of the cooler temperatures, though, Tzakhi decided to travel in the daylight as long as he could, maybe until after noon before he slept. He watched and listened carefully before crossing a wadi, even keeping an eye on Baka for clues. Sometimes a donkey's keen nose and big ears were important assets.

The problem, though, was that Baka had long ago surrendered free will. The caravans made her willing to follow until she dropped of exhaustion. It had probably been years since she passed the point of balking at a stupid human action.

The wide wadi they approached looked safe and dry. Its floor was fine rock-sand, and it was so large and flat, it almost didn't look like a wadi. The fleeting shadows had disappeared, maybe because there were clouds. There was no understanding them, though. Even in a clear sky there was nothing that should have formed those shadows. Surely they were only imagination, and right now, his imagination was tired, so they were gone.

Tzakhi's stomach said it was a little after noon, so he decided to cross the wadi and then find a camping site on the other side. Baka and Matukah must have sensed his weariness, and they picked up the pace. At first it was silent, just a barely noticeable movement in the desert floor. By the time Tzakhi noticed it, a river rose from the trickle in under a minute. The rushing, foamy mud bore down on them when they were about three-quarters of the way across. This was why the donkeys hurried.

Now Tzakhi understood. He ran.

He could see that the speed of the oncoming flood was too great. They'd be overtaken if they continued. They'd be overtaken if they didn't. Two dead donkeys and dead boy in a death wadi.

Tzakhi could swim well, but no swimmer could fight the crushing power of the brown water. "*L'maher, l'maher!*" he called to the donkeys, and they trotted faster alongside him. He was running so fast that he couldn't wave his hands to urge them on, but he yelled for them to go on, not to stay by his side like he'd trained them to do. Both donkeys could make it if they'd leave Tzakhi behind. Matukah galloped on, lighter and younger. But Baka wouldn't.

She almost made it.

The roiling water first pushed Tzakhi to his knees, then slung him forward head first down the wadi, slamming him into Baka's side. Tzakhi grabbed her pack, and together they were washed downstream. Baka kept her head above water, though, and Tzakhi tried to untie her pack so she could swim freely, but the buffeting was too much. A large limb smashed into him, for several seconds turning them into a careening, spinning, twirling tangle of branches, donkey, and boy.

Tzakhi fought upward each time the current sucked him down, and he was sure the limb would force Baka under with its extra weight. Instead, it snagged between two rocks as they were slung around a sharp bend in the wadi. Baka and Tzakhi were crushed together into the limb by the water, but the wedge made them into a small barricade. The water hit them and swirled around.

Baka found purchase, and she began bobbing, lunging, and lurching toward the bank of the wadi. Tzakhi grabbed her tail, kicking with his legs until he, too, began to feel big rocks beneath. The slippery mud made the bank look impossible to climb, but Baka sure-footedly navigated upward. Sometimes she slid, forcing Tzakhi to dodge her weight, but slowly they ascended until they reached the flat sand above.

Tzakhi collapsed, soaked and exhausted.

They'd have to backtrack to find Matukah, and then he'd have to see how much was ruined in Baka's pack. He'd have to build a fire to dry everything and to salvage the grain and as much of the food as possible. He was banged up from hitting rocks and the limb, and he knew he'd be bruised and stiff tomorrow. It would be a long time before he could sleep.

CHAPTER TWENTY-TWO

Most of the scorpions were still alive in their tightly woven little baskets. Once they recovered, he could use the dead ones as food, and the live ones would cannibalize the dead ones. Tzakhi wouldn't have to catch bugs to feed them for a few days.

Tzakhi spread the remaining grain to dry. The ink jar's wax seal didn't seem broken. The parchments he also spread on a warm rock to dry. The sandals would shrink a little, but were fine, and they'd stretch back out when worn. His quiver was full of sandy mud, and so was his shofar.

The yellow dust he'd brought to rub into the donkeys' coats and on his own skin hardened. It could be scraped back into dust, but it would take extra time. Without the yellow dust that accumulated on the ground around the sulfur springs, the biting flies and midges would make Arava summers miserable.

His crisis was the extra water skins that allowed Tzakhi to take the faster route to his destination. The bumping had squeezed out the fresh water and allowed the flood's salty, dirty water to seep in. They had no more drinking water. Even if he refilled them with fresh water, the water in the skins would still taste muddy.

It took over an hour to find Matukah. She was browsing in the brush, nibbling curiously on plants long too dry to be edible. Her pack was mostly empty of his food. He'd seen it bouncing out of the baskets as she galloped ahead of him across the wadi. The steep climb had probably emptied even more. There was no leather top flap to Matukah's light reed pack. There were some roasted nuts in the bottom of the basket, a few pieces of jerky and some dates, and a lot of spilled olive oil.

Baka and Matukah needed water, and so did Tzakhi. When he awoke that evening, Tzakhi left the donkeys among a tumble of boulders and quietly climbed to the top. Once there, he lay flat against the skyline and observed in the dimming light. There. Two long, converging lines of acacia and small tamarisk trees followed a wadi. As the two lines grew closer, the acacias were more sparse, and the tamarisks increased in number and size.

Tzakhi retrieved the donkeys and walked them to the place where the two lines met. A crunchy carpet of spiral pods and wispy, needle-like leaves blanketed the sand beneath the acacias and tamarisks. Taking the scapula of the ox from Baka's pack, Tzakhi began digging.

After ten minutes of shoveling with the shoulder blade, water began seeping into the hole. Tzakhi widened and deepened it, and slowly the water filled his little well. Before Baka could paw in it, Tzakhi tasted it. Bitter, but not too salty. He filled his waterskin and the shallow pot, then invited her to drink.

There wouldn't be enough water to wash his clothes. He'd lost his turban, but then found it tangled around a twig and the pack strap. It was sodden with mud, sand, and debris. So was everything.

How could he get so close and lose his food rations?

While he waited long minutes for the well to refill so he could replenish the waterskins, Tzakhi thought glumly about how this had to change his plans. Even if he found the man-stealers' camp, he didn't have enough food to sustain himself and a donkey while he waited for help to come.

The wolfpack probably turned back when they reached the flooded wadi. The mud was dried on his tunic, turning it stiff in the drier patches. He must look like a drowned sand rat in a pile of tumbleweeds after a flood.

Think, Tzakhi said to himself. What did he have to use? That's what the desert taught you. Use whatever is there.

Tzakhi had mud.

Mud.

Maybe mud was exactly what could work.

CHAPTER TWENTY-THREE

First, he saw a rock with a scorpion on it. The rock marked a trail. The trail led to a cistern. Its dazzling white rock reminded Tzakhi of the strange shelf of white rock at Ein Tzin where he and Salmah called the wolves to dance. The rock was bright white like his namesake, *tzakhakh*. Was this a good sign? A bad one? There were many rock engravings of poisonous animals like snakes and scorpions scattered around, even one of a venomous lizard. Maybe he was about to be surrounded by danger.

The Scorpions' Ascent was a scorpion going up, but the scorpion rock etching was pointing down. He looked down in the narrow, deep ravine. The rock was bright white, but he could see the water. It was slightly green like most desert springs. The water was said to be good, and now Tzakhi and the girls could drink their fill. He could also clean out the waterskins.

Most importantly, he was only a short walk from his destination. The man-stealers could be anywhere close. Abba could be anywhere close. If Baka heard him or even scented him, she might bray. Abba often fed her the grain reward for making the trip up Givat Chatzevah or accompanied her down the givah on her last journey of the day. If Baka scented him, she might expect food or an ear-rub. When Baka was hungry...and she surely was hungry now...she could be heard from a distance of many bowshots.

It was time to stop, to look, to listen. He was either close to a trap or already in it.

CHAPTER TWENTY-FOUR

Tzakhi lay flat in the sand among a loose tumble of sand rock and flint. He'd left Baka and Matukah ground-tied under a wide acacia where they'd camped once the sun began to pour liquid fire down their backs and the sand became oven coals to their feet.

He stretched out the rough piece of fabric across the lower branches to create extra shade. Although he needed to sleep during the heat of the day, first he wanted to scout ahead among the countless waves of sand and rock so when the sun dropped deeply into the west, they could resume travel knowing the situation of the trail.

It was the fourth day, and Tzakhi knew he was close. Scorpions, gazelles, and snakes etched on rocks didn't lay randomly in the wilderness. And if he were close, then there would be guards posted somewhere. They would find concealment to monitor a bottleneck in the trail.

Tzakhi couldn't make a good guess as to where they were and angle his route behind them in the night. Any givah could conceal ten men. There was no secret or stealthy approach here. A night approach would be confusing and lead to wandering unless it was a full moon. Waiting for the moon's white night light to illuminate the way would take too many more days.

Although he'd never been in a robber-hunting party with Avidan, he'd made it a point to be there when the captain gathered the soldiers at the fortress afterward to review the operation. In listening to how Avidan schooled them on what they did right and wrong, it was easy to piece together the best tactics. There was only one choice here.

As he walked back to camp, Tzakhi spotted movement off to his right. He froze for several long seconds before he slowly turned only his head. It took several more seconds to isolate where the movement came from. It was a deadly desert viper, likely out scenting for mice. Vipers lay for hours near a mouse-den, then struck the first and last brave mouse to emerge.

This, Avidan would say, was the *parnasa* of HaShem. Provision.

It was something Tzakhi never thought he'd *need* to know how to do, but the Kushite traders rewarded him for the viper venom he collected. They carried it back to Kush to sell both as poison and for cures.

A Kenite boy taught Tzakhi the trick to catching a desert viper. Grasp him just behind the head as he burrows through the sand. The moving mound of sand signals where to grab. If one grabbed a little ahead of where it looked like the head was, which was counter to every instinct of self-preservation, that was exactly the best place to grab.

So Tzakhi stalked the viper, which had left the protection of rocks to hunt. This viper was not likely to burrow into the sand, though, so Tzakhi picked up a sturdy stick with a nice fork in its end. From afar, the wolves sat and watched, maybe recognizing his hunting posture. They must have waited to make a wiser crossing of the flooded wadi. So much for his own "wise" silver streaks.

The viper only scented and felt his vibration at the last second, and he slithered a few amot before Tzakhi pinned his head with the fork of the stick. Although it fought for a long minute, its undulating muscles eventually calmed enough for Tzakhi to carry it back to camp. Tzakhi's intelligent hand was his left, so he fished in Baka's pack with his right until he found a small clay ointment pot.

He poured the remainder of the lavender ointment in the pot on his own forearms, lower legs, and turban. Next, he set the empty pot on a flat rock, knelt, and held the viper's head to the lip of the vessel until it bit down. Squeezing the viper's venom muscles from either side, Tzakhi milked the venom from its fangs until no more emerged.

Although he had no disagreement with the viper, it was after all, parnasa. He dispatched it, severing its head with his knife. The wolves had moved closer, looking curious. Tzakhi walked out to them, holding the headless snake. "Mother Wolf," he said. "Here is something small for you and your children." He tossed the gift to her. All Tzakhi needed was the venom. He walked back to the camp, rubbing the last of the insect-repelling ointment into his arms and legs.

CHAPTER TWENTY-FIVE

Har Karkom lay dimly in the distance marked by its twin peaks. The Mountain of Saffron. It was situated in the Paran wilderness where Israelites had spent much of their wilderness journey after they left Egypt. Many believed it was Mount Chorev, another name for Mount Sinai, the place where the Israelites received the Torah. Some called it Har HaChag, the Mountain of the Feast. Both people and places often had multiple names. Moshe's Midianite father-in-law had seven names. The Levite had none. Something to think about later.

Whether Har Karkom was really Chorev-Sinai was a matter of debate to be argued over the campfires, but it was surely a sacred site to many peoples. Tzakhi knew without walking across it that it was dotted with many cultic shrines of standing stones for offerings, *matzebot*. There were rock paintings, canyons holding water, and even stone huts for long-term use. Once again the stories of the caravan fires served Tzakhi. He'd drawn maps of faraway places in his head from the time he was only six years old. All he needed was to align what his eyes could see with what his ears had heard.

Karkom was a large mountain plateau with two peaks surrounded by great terraces stepping down into the looser wrinkles of crumbling dry hills and wadis. It was abundant with flint. The isolated peak with the green-water cistern was about an hour's walk away from here. If Abba were being held here, it would be close to a cistern still holding water, concealed from the easy view of travelers or religious pilgrims to this ancient mountain.

Above all, Har Karkom was a mountain with a view. It would be almost impossible to approach without one's movement being detected. A perfect hideout with multiple levels of observation. There were no obvious campers here now, but they would come in winter to observe the solstice with their strange rituals. The crocuses would bloom. Right now was a perfect time to hide out, and here was a perfect place.

After he'd spent some time observing, Tzakhi made his way back, pausing to look at several old campsites marked by make-shift altars, matzebot, and even more drawings on rocks. There were fields of jagged rock and coarse sand. The yellow dust had worn off, and flies pestered him. This hurried him back to where the donkeys were ground-tied in the shade.

He scraped a bit more yellow dust from the hardened mass, rubbed it into the donkeys' coats, and adjusted their brightly knit-ted headdresses. The bright colors were not helpful in camouflag-ing from vigilant eyes, but the fringes agitated the flies away from their voracious feeding on the donkeys' eye fluid.

For himself, Tzakhi had already used the last of the lavender and mint ointment to have use of the vessel, so he also rubbed in some of the smelly yellow dust. Hopefully it would repel any scorpion whose normal hunt-path his camp might block. All three dozed until late afternoon.

After he awoke and ate what was left in the bottom of Matu-kah's basket-pack, Tzakhi prepared. He fed Baka the last of the re-dried barley and allowed her to drink the rest of the water from the waterskins while he went through the pack and removed the parchment and unsealed the ink. He would not burden her with a pack too easy for predators to grab. Tzakhi wrote three words on the parchment:

NACHSHON B'HAR KARKOM

He rolled the parchment tightly into a small, thin patch of oiled leather. Rolling it into a wider patch of oiled leather, and then in another, then in a linen sack. He bound the little roll high into Baka's mane, pulling many strands of mane and forelock into the braid with the linen drawstring. He melted a bit of beeswax and coated the braid, muttering a prayer for it not to melt in the heat.

Tzakhi left Baka's halter without the lead rope and adjusted her fly-bonnet. Hopefully she'd stay at the little spring and eat the grass there like she usually did when ground-tied. "If I'm right, you'll have to go back to the fortress. Be as wise as the wild donkeys of the Negev. I know you'll smell the springs along the way, girl," said Tzakhi. "Drink and eat what you can, but go home fast when I tell you, okay? I have to take Matukah. She won't bray if she hears or smells Abba."

CHAPTER TWENTY-SIX

"**B**oi, Matukah," muttered Tzakhi. He took the lead rope and walked toward unseen watchers. "We're going into the fire."

Tzakhi led Matukah up the trail to the mountain. He knew he was being watched. Such things could be felt in the desert. He wasn't sure about cities. Abba had taken him to Eilat, Be'er Sheva, Arad, and Sela, and the activity overwhelmed him. Here, he could hear everything and see most things. The advantage of the desert was thinking...as long as you didn't think too much.

The desert could make you see or hear shimmering things that weren't there. Or maybe they were. Like Avidan had said, maybe the veil was thin here in the wilderness. Maybe The Levite planted something in his mind with the blessing, but Tzakhi once again saw long, undulating, flying shadows. When he looked up, there was nothing above. Then he saw them again. Moving shadows like small clouds made, but then they were gone. Maybe fear made you see things.

And Tzakhi was scared.

Tzakhi had beaten some of the caked mud out of his tunic and turban with a piece of dried wood bark, but he left much of the mud. He'd hidden The Levite's long knife and Baka's heavier pack beneath some rocks. Over his tunic he'd crisscrossed his flint knife scabbard, bow, muddy quiver, and shofar. Tzakhi needed to look like any other fourteen-year-old boy who'd been orphaned of his father in the desert by a flash flood.

As he walked, Tzakhi could feel why people from far away sometimes came here. There was a Presence. It wasn't like anything Tzakhi had ever known, but those who went to Yerushalayim at the three pilgrimage feasts said the Divine Presence hung over the Temple Mount. It was even over the whole city, just not as strong. It was heavy, like the air weighed more.

The trail up to Har Karkom felt a little like that. All he could compare it to was how sometimes when a caravan left Tamar, something lingered. Some caravans were loaded with interesting people or cargoes. They were as entertaining as the faraway places they came from.

The world passed through Tamar. Different skins, eyes, hair, languages, and talents: singing, acrobatics, knife tricks, juggling, or storytelling. Animals of odd shapes or colorful feathers, like monkeys or fan-tailed birds carried from Etzion-Geber to Yerushalayim for Melekh Shlomo's menagerie. Sometimes there was a caravan full of dangerous characters, those quick with a fist or a knife, sometimes pedaling herbs of mystical powers or pulling from their wine jugs too long.

Caravans might depart, but if they'd camped for an extended number of days, often their presence remained. Similarly, here was a lingering Presence, but not quite of people. It was something a little heavier than the usual air. If this was the ancient Mount Sinai, then Tzakhi understood why the Israelites stood far off from it and trembled, even told Moshe they felt like they were dying. Tzakhi sincerely hoped he was not about to die.

The stories told around the caravan and soldiers' fires at night could serve him now. They'd long entertained him, and now he'd have to *be* the story and storyteller. Fortunately, silent Matukah wouldn't be able to contradict him. And The Levite said it was okay to tell a lie if it saved a life. Tzakhi needed to save Abba's life and his own.

Tzakhi stopped several times, pretending to look about as if not sure which direction to go. He even turned back in the direction from which he came and studied the horizon and the sun. Although Matukah would follow him without a lead rope, he kept a firm hold on it and started walking southward again. And then, Matukah pricked her dark ears and looked upward toward one of the shelves of the mountain plateau. A long shriek echoed across the sand and rock from above.

It was the greeting bray of a mule, high and shrill, not like the long, low, bellows-like rhythm of a donkey. Matukah didn't bray back, but she started pulling in the direction of the mule, which Tzakhi couldn't see yet, but he could hear plainly. A mule wasn't the usual choice. It might be a mount for the wealthy to ride. Or a baggage animal for soldiers who traveled at a faster pace on horse-back than camels.

Tzakhi affected an interested look and let Matukah guide him toward the mule. At some point, Tzakhi knew someone had fallen in behind him. The wolves and Avidan had taught him to sense when someone...or something...was on his flank.

When he gained a shelf of the plateau, he was quickly sur-rounded. A young Egyptian held the lead rope of a mule loaded with water-skins. In the not-too-far distance were two stone huts and a campfire. Men closed in on him from either side and behind. Tzakhi stopped and looked around, reading their clothes and hairstyle.

Amalekites.

CHAPTER TWENTY-SEVEN

Amalekites hated Israelites, especially those of the tribes of Judah and Shimon who lived in the Negev, thwarting their brutal raiding on caravans and small villages. Melekh Shlomo had placed over fifty outposts in the Negev and Arava to control the Amalekites' raiding.

That explained much. It explained who designed the desert escape plan, who had known much about the wilderness lands of the Arava and Negev, and who had killed Abba's bodyguards so precisely. Amalekites were master planners of ambush and unspeakable atrocities against their targets. No matter who was paying the man-stealers, Abba was in the worst hands possible.

There were two other men, not Amalekites, and two Edomites. One of them was the one who'd followed him from behind.

Sar Hadad was easy to identify. He wore Egyptian clothing and a short bob of hair even though he was not wearing any specific identification of the royal household, just a plain gold bracelet and necklace. Clean-shaven.

There was one, though, that Tzakhi could not identify. Unlike Sar Hadad's short, even hair, the strange man was paler, wore long, flowing hair, and had a pointed beard. His clothes were mixed of fabric and skins. The curly hair was capped by a form-fitting fabric turban that required no wrapping. His weapons were crafted unlike those of any land Tzakhi knew.

One of the Amalekites grabbed Matukah's lead rope from Tzakhi. "What are you doing here?" he asked in his Canaanite language.

Tzakhi answered him in the same language, "My father and I were caught in a flash flood. He and his donkey were swept away along with all our trade goods. My donkey ran ahead, and I was caught by a limb. I was able to climb out, but I lost most of our food, and the water was ruined."

Sar Hadad...if the older Egyptian was Sar Hadad...seemed to understand the language, but he could tell the strange man didn't. Sar Hadad translated from Canaanite into a strange language for the other. It sounded vaguely familiar, but Tzakhi didn't know it. Yavan? Kittim? They rarely traveled through Tamar, preferring instead to trade on the coast with the sons of Nevaiot, the Nabateans.

"So what led you here?" asked Sar Hadad.

"I heard of the white cistern, and hoped there would be water enough for me to wash and fill the water-skins. Then I could go toward Seir and find the closest outpost, maybe Karka or Adar," said Tzakhi. He added, pointing toward the mule carrying the water-skins, "The water left in the wadi was just mud. You're here, so there must still be fresh water."

"Odd that you'd get caught in a flash flood this time of year," commented an Edomite.

"We saw the clouds, but we, too, didn't think they held water this time of year," said Tzakhi. "And they were far away. But we were wrong."

The men were silent for a moment, probably remembering the cloud cover as well.

"Where are you from?" asked Sar Hadad, who scrutinized the hem of Tzakhi's tunic. Even though muddy, the Israelite tzitziyot fringes were visible.

"Since my ima died, my abba carries messages and does trading among the oases and caravansaries," said Tzakhi. "He looks for specific things if people want them. We travel all the time."

"Like what?" asked the dark Edomite.

"Particular types of precious stones or seashells, maybe clay molds or a piece of carving ivory. Seeds or dyes or leaves for cures. Whatever a person will want, Abba seeks. *Did* seek." Tzakhi tried to look very sad. "Everything we were carrying was lost with him in the flood. I have only a few things left to sell for food, but if you can spare enough food for me to make it to an outpost, I'd be grateful. Maybe some dates or pistachios."

One of the Amalekites rummaged unashamedly through Matukah's light packsaddle. "What's in these little baskets?" he asked, removing one of the scorpion cages.

"Fighting scorpions," said Tzakhi. "For gambling."

The Amalekite flung the basket on the ground like it was a furnace coal.

Tzakhi went on, "The soldiers like to fight them. Sometimes we trade in the Negev outposts. It is quite a lonely job, so they are always looking for amusements. Would you like to gamble? Those are fine fighters."

His question went unanswered.

Sar Hadad and the stranger conversed for several minutes, and the men waited. Tzakhi was not told, but he knew, that he would not be allowed to leave the spot where he and Matukah stood unless the two in charge said so.

The beardless young Egyptian flashed him a sympathetic look and led the mule away. He disappeared so quickly that Tzakhi realized there must be a trail downward, maybe where they kept their horses. These were horsemen, Tzakhi was sure. You could tell by the way they walked.

After some back-and-forth in the strange language with the strange man, Sar Hadad gave the Amalekites and Edomites a dismissive look. He said to Tzakhi, "My friend here from Kittim and I were on a trade mission from Egypt to Melekh Shlomo. We traveled back to make an offering at Har Sin before we crossed into Egypt, but the official in our party has fallen ill. He is recovering in one of the huts, and we are waiting for him to be well enough to travel. Clean up, stay the night, and we'll get you some food and you can fill your waterskins before you're on your way."

"Thank you, adoni,"[30] said Tzakhi. He would not be given extra food or water until they decided to send him away. An invisible rope.

"You speak Egyptian?" Sar Hadad asked.

"Yes, adoni. I speak several languages I learned from trading," answered Tzakhi in Egyptian.

"Don't try to leave without telling us," warned Sar Hadad. "The Kitti and his official are important. They are both under the protection of Pharaoh, so the Edomite and Amalekite soldiers watch the coming and going closely. We wouldn't want harm to come to the official. It's bad enough that he's fallen ill. Even Melekh Shlomo would be angry if he died."

"I understand, adoni," said Tzakhi. *Nice story. Better than mine.*

Sar Hadad nodded to one of the Amalekites. The men had relaxed, but the Amalekite ran his hands over Tzakhi, searching for any hidden weapons. When he finished, he clapped his hands

---

30 "my lord," or "sir"

together to remove some of the pale mud before he held his hands out. "Give me the bow and quiver."

Tzakhi obediently handed them over.

"You can have them back when you leave," said Sar Hadad. "Keep your flint knife."

"When my slave returns from watering the horses," said Sar Hadad, "he'll show you the cistern where you can wash. Make sure you stay out of the pool of drinking water. It's hard to tell the difference between you and the desert."

CHAPTER TWENTY-EIGHT

Tzakhi didn't like the way one of the Amalekites looked at him, but he walked down to the bathing pool anyway. The Amalekite followed him all the way down. It didn't feel safe to remove his tunic or get into the water, but Tzakhi wasn't sure what to do about it. In his gut, he felt like he should run as far as he could from the man. The man's smile was the smile of many sheidim preparing to feed on a demoniac.

The Amalekite's eyes grew with a desire Tzakhi had seen in those who sought out the Edomite trader's tent near the Tamar fortress. It was a sheen burnished by darkest evil. It was a sheen that didn't care who it hurt. It was a sheen that didn't care about anything but satisfying the sheid. And it glowed with more than desire. It was murderous.

The man tried too hard to sound harmless when he called out to Tzakhi. It was like when the drovers tried to catch a reluctant camel or donkey in the big pens. What they really wanted to do was whip the animal into compliance, but instead they faked a soothing, assuring tone. It never fooled the animals, and it didn't fool Tzakhi. This man was about to do something very bad to him.

Suddenly, there was a strong gust of sandy wind, a whirlwind. It was odd. Whirlwinds formed on the desert floor, not in the cisterns. It silently enveloped the Amalekite, who clutched at his eyes and yelled. He couldn't move out of it. No matter where the Amalekite moved, the whirlwind moved. Strange shadows moved along the canyon wall, and Tzakhi looked up, expecting to see hawks, but there was nothing.

Staggering toward the water, the Amalekite stumbled and fell in, screaming again when his foot wedged into the rocks and he couldn't pull it loose. Instead, his wrenching made him fall repeatedly on the stones. Just as suddenly as it appeared, the whirlwind dissipated, and the swirling shadows disappeared as well.

By the time the others slid down the bank to help, the Amalekite had mangled himself. The knee of the tethered leg twisted at a strange angle, and the other knee was a mass of swelling red bruises from banging it on the rock. So were his arms, especially his elbows. His eyes were closed in agony, occasionally opening blindly, and he snaked his neck back and forth as if trying to escape some pain behind his eyes.

When the others tried to grab him and steady him long enough to release his foot, he fought like a madman, screaming, drooling, and tearing at his clothes. It took all of them working together to secure his arms and the free leg so they could remove the trapped one. When they finally led him to the bank, he fell, nearly naked, bleeding from self-inflicted scratches and writhing in pain.

"No one would ever know," the man began sobbing. "Who would know? They would only think he was drowned in the flood with his father. I could have drowned him, too..."

The Kitti pulled his knife and slit the man's throat cleanly. The others said nothing, not even the other Amalekites. "Which one of you knew he was a madman?" asked the Kitti coldly in heavily accented Egyptian. "And failed to tell me?"

The Amalekites looked at each other in befuddlement. "We didn't know," one finally answered, also in Egyptian. "Maybe it was the heat. The heat sickness makes people do strange things. He would have been okay if we'd given him water and put him in the shade."

"That wasn't heat sickness," said the Kitti. "What we must do, we must do with precision. I should reduce the price of your payment for endangering the..." The Kitti looked over at Tzakhi.

Tzakhi looked back blankly, the way he'd learned to do with caravan merchants asking more than anyone would ever give for the product.

"This ragged cub may be of use to us," said Sar Hadad. "And if he wants to eat our food, then he must work."

What did he mean? Tzakhi wasn't sure what kind of work he could do in such a camp.

Sar Hadad said, "Our horses need water every day. The wadi is dry this time of year. You and your donkey will pack water from the cistern down to their trough. There is a cache of hay, oats, and barley near the top of the wadi. You will feed the horses each day and keep the trough full. My slave will show you how much to feed. He's the other Egyptian. You can speak Egyptian or Canaanite with him."

"My donkey is only two years old," said Tzakhi. "She has not yet carried that much weight."

"The work will help her grow," said the Kitti dismissively, "and if you want her to eat as well, she will work."

Tzakhi nodded.

"Now wash yourself," said Sar Hadad. "Then take the donkey down to the wadi with the horses before her manure attracts more flies to the camp."

CHAPTER TWENTY-NINE

After the midnight watch changed, Tzakhi crept from the sleeping hut. He waited until the last shift was sleeping soundly. The night watch would not yet have sensed all the night rhythms.

The moon was almost full, but clouds helped him. Or at least they were kind of like clouds. The shadows moved languorously across the camp, seeming to crisscross overhead sometimes. They kept Tzakhi's movements concealed in their odd shadows.

Now that he knew where the guards were stationed relative to his last camp, Tzakhi moved slowly until he reached the visual perimeter of the watchers' posts. A shadow passed overhead, maybe a small cloud covering the moon. When the northern guard turned and looked up, Tzakhi slipped between him and the eastern guard. He chose a slow path through an in-between area too dim to be seen from either post clearly.

Once he found cover in the seams of the sand and rock, Tzakhi used them to speed back to the camp where Baka waited. He desperately prayed she wouldn't bray, but he'd purposely positioned her far enough away that the sound shouldn't carry. Still, the shadows and sounds in this place had an odd quality to them.

Baka had heard or scented his coming, but she didn't bray. She stood expectantly, sure he had some barley or a treat. "Here, girl," said Tzakhi. "All I could manage was a few dates." He adjusted her fly-bonnet and halter, then gave her a liberal ear-scratching while she ate the sweets.

Tzakhi didn't have the time to waste in case one of the others got up to pass water and noticed him missing. Carefully, Tzakhi checked to make sure the parchment roll was secure. "You must go home, okay, Baka? As fast as you can."

Baka pushed at him with her head, hoping for more ear-scratching or hidden treats.

Tzakhi pulled her around by the halter, pointing her northeast toward Tamar. He slapped her lightly on the rump. "*L'bayitah, Baka, l'bayitah! L'maher, l'maher!*"

CHAPTER THIRTY

Within a day, Tzakhi understood the layout of the camp and most of its men. He was sure it was Abba who was held in one of the two stone huts. Two guards were posted there at all times, working in day and night shifts. Sar Hadad explained the sick man might be contagious, and couldn't be allowed contact. Only the four guards had contact with him. If he improved, their band would move on. If not, they'd bury him and then return to Egypt.

The explanation for their military-style band that they'd been on a mission from Pharaoh to Melekh Shlomo, then rode to Har Sin to sacrifice to the moon god was not a bad one. The mountain was not far from Karkom, so the explanation was plausible, but Tzakhi did not believe it. He knew Abba was inside the hut, not a sick Egyptian. He knew it for sure because Abba's sturdy Hittite horse was among the man-stealers' fleet Egyptian mounts.

Brilliantly, they had concealed all their horses from the sight of other travelers. From the remains of camps, altars, and matzebot scattered from peak to peak and plateau to plateau, Tzakhi could see that those who worshiped here gave one another lots of space. Perhaps people had particular altars they returned to year after year.

Horses, however, would be remarkable in this place. Certainly the Amalekites had located the wadi where the horses were hidden from sight. Amalekites were good at popping up out of the desert with no warning. They knew its every seam.

The wadi was fenced with rocks and flood debris at two narrow bends. Twenty horses and some mules stood in groups of two or three around small piles of hay. A shallow trough was hewn out of soft stone. It lay slightly askew on the bank of the wadi, elevated, but accessible. Just a little higher up, the bank was too steep for a horse to navigate. A narrow game path followed a less steep access up the side of the wadi, but only one horse at a time could safely use the trail. It, too, was blocked off.

Tzakhi guessed the wadi was often used as a corral, perhaps to hold the donkeys or camels of worshipers, or maybe to hold the sheep and goats for sacrifices at the many small altars Tzakhi had seen. A damp place suggested it held water for some months after the rains, but not enough for animals to water this late in the year. The man-stealers were packing water down to the trough. Well, the Egyptian youth was packing it. Now it was Tzakhi and Matukah.

Tzakhi desperately needed to talk to Avidan. He needed a plan, whether for sabotage or battle, he wasn't certain. He didn't know if his message would reach Tamar. He didn't know if his brief note would be enough to point a search party along the right path. If Avidan, yes. There was no other logical path out of Karkom. If the man-stealers intended to escape to Egypt, they'd already be there. East to Timna was a copper curtain. There was only one way to miss the Negev outposts. Scorpions' Ascent. North.

Avidan's practical voice always cut through the noise of Tzakhi's "What ifs...?" even if it was Avidan proposing the "What if...?"

What do you see, Tzakhi? Describe the defensive formation of the enemy.

"About twenty horsemen according to the number of horses. Well, less one Amalekite. Two baggage mules. Enough fodder to sustain the horses for about a week. Trail rations are already packed so they can leave quickly. Each man has a ration pack prepared beside his saddle-cloth."

What does that tell you?

"They'll probably move Abba within a week."

Scouts? Watchers? Messengers?

"There are four men watching the four directions, one or two moving between them collecting information, carrying messages, or bringing them food and water. They work in twelve-hour shifts, noon to midnight or midnight to noon. One watch is Amalekites, and the other is Edomites. The night watch pulls in closer to the camp."

How do you think they'll travel?

"It's hard to say..."

Don't waste my time.

"I think the day and night watchers form two squads of six. Sar Hadad, the Kitti, the young Egyptian, and Abba's guards form a third squad of six. That will be the one escorting him. Two squads will go ahead, each with a pack mule. One will go a day's journey, and the other one will go another day's journey farther. They'll give their horses a day of rest and fill waterskins from a village or outpost cistern.

As the escort squad comes near the village in the night, they will trade with the advance squad for the fresher horses and re-supply with water and rations. Although it might take them four days to reach a seaport, their horses can travel the last couple of days without re-supply."

Do you see any weaknesses in that plan?

"It depends upon their horses and mules being sound enough to make the journey. If they are missing one horse, or one is not as rested as the others, it will slow the entire squad. But each squad could lose a few men without it hindering the speed and security of their travel. Sick or injured men would slow them down more... at least disrupt their thinking."

Any other weaknesses?

"There's only one trail out of the horse wadi. If they needed to move fast, it would take a lot of time for them all to mount up."

And?

If one of the outposts had word of the real identity of the riders, then soldiers could intervene. The outposts communicate with signals of smoke and messenger doves."

Do they know that?

"Of course. Especially the Amalekites. The outposts are to keep them from attacking the cities of Shimon and Yehudah and the caravans."

Then who would be the loose end that might notify an outpost of the riders?

I am.

CHAPTER THIRTY-ONE

Baka trotted across a wadi. She could smell brackish water. Behind her, two wolves followed. Predators. Danger. She switched her tail at them, warning them she would kick them, stomp them, and then shake them by the neck until dead. They seemed to know how close they could get. They didn't harm the boy, but predators were predators.

Hungry. She was hungry. The boy fed her twice a day, more if she made multiple trips up the givah. She hadn't eaten more than a bit of dry desert grass in two days. The spring water at the fortress was sweet, not like the moisture she scented in the stale little seep at the bottom of the wadi. It smelled like a shallow, dank pool where a few birds would wet their beaks.

She was close to home. Home was sweet water and barley. Sometimes a barley and date-honey mash or an armful of grass hay. Plenty of barley hay and treats of sweet dates. Shade under the tamarisk trees and other donkeys to exchange brays of greeting.

The stiff desert breeze shifted, and her nostrils filtered another odor. Sheep. Soon, her long ears swiveled, picking up the sound of bleating sheep and the weaker mews of the lambs. Sheep muddied the waters. Sheep meant humans. She'd not seen humans for two days, not since the boy gave her the command to go home to the water trough. To hurry.

Baka made a sharp turn in the wadi, and there was the small pool. And there were the sheep. A small herd. Muddy water. But water. Baka stopped and sniffed for the scent of humans. She could smell them, but she couldn't see them. A few sheep bleated at her and stared, but she ignored them. Lowering her head, she made her way through the small herd and tried the water. Yes, brackish and muddied, but water. Moving a few more feet into the deeper part of the pool where the water was cleaner, she shouldered the sheep aside.

Human voices approached from behind the rocks. Her nose told her they'd relieved themselves. Two humans. Sheep-men, not caravan men. Not furnace-men. Not horsemen. They smelled of their sheep. The men noticed her. Baka looked up, allowing the green water to stream from her muzzle. The men spoke to one another. Baka went back to the water and finished drinking.

The water was warm, but it felt good to her hooves. A nap in the protection of the sheep herd would be nice, but when she tried to graze a bit near the pool, the sheep-men shouted at her, moving her away. There wasn't much grazing here, and the sheep had already stripped away much. Better to trot on home. She was close. Food was there. A safe stall to sleep in at night.

Baka turned her nose to the wind, scenting. One of the sheep-men approached. Did he have barley? Suddenly, he grabbed her halter and gave a shout to the other sheep-man. It was a glad shout. He jerked on her halter. This confused her. She was supposed to go home. Home to food. Home to water. Home to the boy's care. Kind words. The last human who'd jerked on her neck like this was the one who beat her.

She reared a little, throwing her weight against his hand, then shied backward to break free, but the second sheep-man approached and also grabbed for her halter. Confusion. Obey the human. But not these humans. She must go home. Food. Water. A safe place to sleep. Kind words.

The second sheep-man held the other side of her halter, securing her, but not before clumsily ripping her bonnet away. The itchy bonnet keeping away the eye-biters. The itch was not as bad as the stings. Baka tried again to break away, but the sheep-men had leverage now. When the humans held her securely, she must give up. There was no getting away now. If she struggled more, she would be beaten.

Baka then smelled the danger close. They raced around the rocks, scattering the sheep both directions of the wadi. The wolves.

The sheep-men turned to see, and then shouted again. The wolves were not chasing the sheep. They stopped in front of the sheep-men, raising their hair and growling, snarling. White teeth. Their fronts crouched low, eyes narrow, preparing to leap. Baka would have protected the boy. Not these men shouting at her like caravan drovers. All she wanted now was to go home. Home where there was food. Fresh water. Hay to munch. Shade to doze in. A safe place to sleep at night.

Baka lowered her head, squatted, pulled, and broke away. She galloped through the sheep and scrambled up the side of the wadi. Once she'd gained the desert floor, she looked back. The men were frozen by the snapping wolves, unable to move.

The wolves swung their gazes up at her, and then together they retreated, turned, and chased down the wadi after the scattered sheep. This sped the retreat of the terrified herd. The sheep-men would not leave their sheep. One of them pulled a slingshot and searched for a stone, but the wolves were quickly out of sight. Baka set her face toward home and trotted faster than the humans could run.

Home. Food. Fresh water. A doze in the shade.

CHAPTER THIRTY-TWO

Tzakhi's mental conversation with Avidan helped. First of all, he'd need to escape to an outpost at just the right time, or they'd hurry their departure. He'd lose any possibility of Avidan reaching them in time. But if he didn't escape fast enough, the Kitti would kill him. Their horses were faster than Matukah, and much faster than his feet. He was very sure of that.

Tzakhi was not willing to hamstring the horses, at least not yet. It might be possible to use his iron hoof-trimming tool to quick them. To do that, he'd trim away enough of the horn-like hoof material until he reached the sensitive part. When the horse took a step, especially if he carried the weight of a burden, the pain prevented him from moving. It was like a hangnail on the bottom of one's foot.

It was a mistake occasionally made in trimming horses and donkeys, but better than allowing overgrown hooves to split and break, which would lame them for sure. The effects only lasted a day or two. That was not practical, though. Even if the horses would let him do it without someone holding a lead rope, it would take too long to quick them all.

He must use everything the desert offered him.

And most importantly, a prayer to HaShem.

CHAPTER THIRTY-THREE

Tzakhi squatted next to the Egyptian's slave, who was stirring a porridge of barley and lentils. He'd finished feeding and watering the horses for the day. At the slave's nod, Tzakhi poured another measure of water into the kettle. As he poured, Tzakhi wondered if Baka made it to Tamar. It had been three days.

Each passing day he was denied travel, but he was worked and fed.

One of the Amalekite watchers lay nearby in the shade of the sleeping hut. He was consumed with a fever, and his foot was swelling, breaking open into a purple and bloody wound. He sometimes half-heartedly swatted at the flies congregating under a cloth the slave had placed over it, but Tzakhi could tell there was enough dead flesh that soon maggots would emerge.

Two nights ago, the Amalekite had gone out of the hut in the night to pass water and stepped on a porcupine quill. The infection was evident by morning. The sandy desert floor concealed all kinds of treasures and curses. Only time could reveal them.

Last night, another Amalekite had been stung on the inner thigh as he slept. Although no one had been able to locate the culprit in the darkness, Tzakhi strongly suspected the offender was a black fat-tailed scorpion. They were strong fighters in the gambling box. Tzakhi had made sure to coat himself in the yellow dust before going to sleep.

That Amalekite also lay in the shade of the hut, the venom spreading from a round swelling. It radiated red streaks through his upper leg and lower abdomen. The man was sweating, occasionally vomiting, even drooling a little. He could no longer walk, and at times, he spoke to things no one else could see or swatted at things in the air. There was some muttering among the Amalekite squad that they'd come under a curse.

A heavy foot thudded into Tzakhi's back, propelling him toward the fire. He broke his fall with his hands and scrambled backward, panicking at the nearness of the flames. A hand grabbed the back of his tunic and lifted him powerfully. This time he was dumped hard onto his back in the sand.

The Kitti and Sar Hadad looked as shocked as the Egyptian slave and the other five men awaiting a cooked meal.

"I remember you now," said one of the Edomites. "It took a few days, but now I remember. Your father is no trader. He's very much alive. Your father is in that hut over there."

Tzakhi sat up, stomach sinking.

"You're Nachson's youngest son. You live at Tamar," the Edomite continued.

Sar Hadad looked at Tzakhi curiously, then back at the Edomite. "How do you know that?"

"When Nahat and I were scouting Tamar with the caravan, I saw this boy. He worked the caravan, but the slave trader said he was Nachshon's son...maybe," said the Edomite.

"Why 'maybe'?" asked the Kitti.

"His hair. Nachshon's sons have red hair. This one's hair is turning white. He's cast some spell over us. We're down three men since he arrived."

They all looked at Tzakhi. No sense in denying it, at least the hair part. He couldn't change his hair color. The Edomite snatched the turban from Tzakhi's head, and his silver streaks fell around his shoulders. He was long overdue for a haircut, and although tightly curled, his long pe-ot fell all the way past his collar-bone.

Sar Hadad said, "Son of a..."

"Wolf," finished the Kitti.

"Wolf?" asked Sar Hadad, looking confused.

The Kitti nodded. His eyes did not size up Tzakhi like the caravan traders figuring small margins. His eyes were like a gambler's who knows he has a winning play, a trader who need not trade, for what he holds is worth far more than what he might win. "Have you ever heard the oracle of the Kittim?" the Kitti asked Tzakhi.

"No, adoni," said Tzakhi.

"You have not heard the Prophecy of Latium and its twins?"

"No, adoni."

"Nothing of Romulus and Remus who will come?"

"Who?" asked Tzakhi.

"Romulus and Remus. The twins who will be born and rule a great city along the Tiber River. Romulus will one day rule the world."

Tzakhi shook his head, and the other men looked curious. All except for Sar Hadad, whose eyes glittered in sudden comprehension of something. He looked at Tzakhi with new interest. "Remus has the hair of the silver she-wolf, his adopted mother. It is the oracle."

The Kitti laughed a very cold laugh. "I thought I found Nachshon, the world's greatest armorer, but I found the father of Remus. Should I kill you now and return your silver head to Latium, or should I carry you there alive for a ceremonial death and feast to celebrate the victory of Romulus rising?'"

Tzakhi said nothing. He was no one's father. Abba hadn't betrothed him to anyone. It was something that usually happened for his brothers on a pilgrimage feast after they'd worked for a few years in the mines and were ready for a steady post. This Kitti might be as mad as his Amalekite friend. But it was undeniable that the Kitti wanted to make Tzakhi the guest of honor at a feast for his own death. For now, he was very glad that he wasn't pushed back toward the fire.

There must have been silence for a full minute. This was Sar Hadad's command, but everyone feared the Kitti more. Including Tzakhi. The Kitti spoke again.

"Who knows you're here, boy?"

"No one. No one would come. All the soldiers who were left were deployed in the direction of Ashur. I sneaked by the guards at night because I didn't believe the scouts," said Tzakhi. "The attack sounded to me like Amalekites, not Ashuri cavalry. I've lived my whole life here. The soldiers left at the fortress don't understand the Arava."

"You're a liar, but I believe that," said Sar Hadad. "And what did you think you'd do if you found us?"

"Maybe...maybe let one of the outposts know so they'd send soldiers," Tzakhi answered.

"That won't happen," said the Kitti.

"Why didn't you go to an outpost when you saw us?" asked Sar Hadad.

"I did have the accident in the flash flood. I lost all my rations and water. Once I saw you were here, I didn't have enough food or water for the donkey and me to walk to an outpost," said Tzakhi.

The Kitti contemplated Tzakhi's answer, sizing him up. Finally he said to the slave, "Take away his knife, tie him up, and hobble him, but keep him away from his father. I will decide by morning whether to take the boy or just his head back to Latium. If his father has heard him...and surely he has...and he knows I killed him, he will be much harder to manage on the journey. I may take the boy along as leverage. If Nachshon doesn't reveal the secrets and turn out good armor, we'll torture the boy until he does. Nachshon should appreciate how a good fire can change things."

Sick to his stomach at the words, Tzakhi removed his knife scabbard by its sling and placed it on the ground. He didn't want them to think he'd resist.

The Kitti picked up the scabbard and unsheathed the flint knife. "You made this?" he asked Tzakhi conversationally.

"Yes, adoni," said Tzakhi.

Nodding, the Kitti walked over to the Amalekites. He slit the throat of the drooling one, which caused the one with the rotting foot to try to run away. The Kitti patiently walked after him, gaining ground each time the Amalekite fell. He didn't make it even a half bowshot away before he met the same end as the first. As with the crazy Amalekite at the cistern, it made Tzakhi nauseated. "You like that?" asked the Kitti when he returned.

"No, adoni," said Tzakhi.

"Then you are a sick boy. You should like it. My way was much faster than the slow, suffering death you inflicted upon them. It is proper I used your knife. It is kinder."

Tzakhi had nothing to say to that.

The Kitti grabbed Tzakhi's hair and pulled it upward tautly, stretching his neck. Tzakhi closed his eyes and waited. He tried to tell himself it was better than the fire, but fear froze the thought.

Instead of feeling his throat sliced, the knife tugged sharply on the top of his hair. Tzakhi opened his eyes and looked, and the Kitti held one of his silver locks. Thankfully, not his pe-ot. Tzakhi wasn't superstitious, but he supposed every Israelite man guarded his pe-ot a little more carefully after they heard what Delilah did to Shimshon.

The Kitti tossed the knife to the slave and put the hair inside his neck pouch. *What was that for?*

"We don't have enough men to guard him tonight unless we bind him hand and foot," said Sar Hadad. "And we definitely don't want him inside the hut with us. The boy is a silent killer. Perhaps he does use sorcery."

No sorcery, thought Tzakhi. *Just ancient desert-craft*. At this moment, however, a long-bodied wing-shadow swooped low over them, making everyone look up for an eagle, hawk, or vulture. There was nothing, or it turned too suddenly to spot it. Tzakhi didn't know what it was, but why not instill a little doubt? Let them think *sheidim* had invaded their camp. He gave the men a small smile and held out his hands for the rope as if that's exactly what he'd come there for.

"The messenger will rotate him through the four watch stations tonight. Each watcher will guard him for three hours on the watch so we don't need to wonder what kind of spells he's casting in the night with his scorpions," said the Kitti.

Sar Hadad looked at his slave. "Walk him out to the southern post and leave instructions to watch him."

CHAPTER THIRTY-FOUR

The slave walked Tzakhi to the eastern guard post. "You shouldn't have come here," said the young man. "These are very bad men. Not just the Kitti. The others are restrained because he is the most evil. Don't antagonize them."

"I didn't have a choice," said Tzakhi. "The flood took almost everything. And he's my father. I've already lost my mother."

"The Kitti and Sar Hadad don't care about that. Sar Hadad lost his father to Melekh David in the war between Edom and Israel. He would kill your father in revenge if he didn't need his iron secrets. You'd better have some secrets of your own if you wish to survive."

"I'm not a sorcerer," said Tzakhi. "I'm not a sheid, either."

"I know," said the Egyptian.

"How do you know that?" asked Tzakhi curiously.

"The shadows. The madness. The scorpion's sting to the Amalekite's thigh. It's the tzirah, not you. You may have put the scorpion in his blanket, but the scorpion knew where to sting. The tzirah attacks eyes or thighs."

Tzakhi was surprised. "You know of the tzirah?"

The Egyptian paused, perhaps to see if someone else might be listening. "Yes," he finally said. "The tzirah attacks Egypt at certain times of the year. The only defense is the ibis. That's why it's sacred to Egyptians."

"Ibis?" asked Tzakhi skeptically. How could a frail bird protect against a supernatural creature? No one was sure exactly what the tzirah was. Serpent? Scorpion? Locust? Hornet?

The Egyptian said, "I know. It doesn't make sense. The priests have their reasons. Their gods."

"'Their gods?' Not your gods? You don't seem like the others," Tzakhi commented.

"I'm Sar Hadad's slave," he said. "Not a fool." He switched to Hebrew, "*Ain od m'ilvado*. There is only one God."

This, too, surprised Tzakhi. Maybe he should have noticed the slave's speech was slightly accented. "You are an Israelite?"

"Yes," said the slave. "I am neither Canaanite nor Egyptian. My father died in battle, then my mother died. I was sold for the debts, and there was no one to redeem me. I was traded three times because I was too young to do heavy work. It was a small debt, but I was a small boy."

"But you're Hebrew," said Tzakhi. "Your work should never have been sold for more than six years."

"Each time I traded hands, the purchaser of my debt was less scrupulous. After I was sold to an Egyptian, there was no distinction. I was taken to Egypt and traded again twice more. I'd changed hands six times before I was twelve. Sar Hadad kept me as his valet."

"Does he know you're...?"

"No," said the young man. "I say Shema silently. I never speak Hebrew. Sar Hadad thinks I'm Canaanite, just sold too young to remember my parents."

"I'm sorry," said Tzakhi.

"I'm sorry, too," said the slave. "You and your abba are in a very bad place."

Tzakhi hobbled alongside, but the slave considerately kept a slow pace. "What is your name?" asked Tzakhi.

"Shua."

"I'm Tzakhi."

"*Naim meod.*"

"*Naim meod.*"

"Shua?"

"Yes?"

"Stay near the hut tonight. Don't enter the fight."

"I will. And I won't." Shua bumped into Tzakhi, taking the moment to place a sharp flint between his bound hands, then resumed their walk.

"And one more thing, Shua. If you are willing..."

CHAPTER THIRTY-FIVE

Tzakhi sat with his back to a large rock. His guard had a routine, which is never good. He walked a slow circle around the rock on his post, looking into the night, listening, but never varying his route, never talking to Tzakhi, only glancing. The guards changed around midnight, and the new guard's routine was much the same. It took only about thirty minutes after the midnight guard change for Tzakhi to cut through the ropes binding his hands. He needed only a few minutes more to release the hobbles on his feet.

He waited for the messenger to make his rounds and speak with his watcher before moving on for a report from the north watch. Afterward, Tzakhi's watcher resumed his pace. As he made his left turn around the rock, Tzakhi crept behind him, stalking, and then flipped one of the empty ropes over the guard's head. He tightened and held, refusing to let go while the man thrashed and pulled at his throat. Years of lifting heavy burdens onto camels and donkeys had made Tzakhi's arms and legs strong in spite of his slim build. So had the extra year. *Thank you, Abba.*

Tzakhi waited until the man went limp. Quickly, he tied him hand and foot, stopping a couple of times to make sure the man was still breathing. Just as the man started to stir, Tzakhi tore the hem of the man's tunic and stuffed it in his mouth. Reaching for the guard's short sword, Tzakhi removed it from its scabbard. The guard's eyes widened, seeing the glint of the metal even in the darkness.

Because he was bound, the guard could do nothing but writhe when Tzakhi cut the tendons of both ankles. Maybe he wouldn't hamstring the horses, but it didn't bother Tzakhi too much to cripple the man-stealer. Now he had a sword. If he worked behind the messenger, he could do his work before the messenger made it back here. Four out of twenty men...make it five out of twenty men...were now out of the fight. He could take out four more within the next hour, *b'azrat HaShem*.[31]

Taking the bound guard's bow, Tzakhi tested the draw. It was not too difficult to bend. From beneath his tunic, he removed the tiny juglet which he'd bound with a thin leather thong next to the copper amulet Shira had given him. He re-broke the wax seal. One by one, he dipped each arrow in the viper venom. It had worked nicely on the porcupine quill.

**

The next morning, the men trickled out of the sleep hut, careful not to exit without sandals securely strapped to their feet. The day messenger scanned the morning haze, looking for his companion on the night shift. It was eerily quiet. He went back into the hut and nudged the Egyptian slave with a toe. "Food," growled the messenger.

Shua roused himself and began setting out the clay plates of jerked meat, dried fruit, and nuts. Not long afterward, the morning silence was explained.

---

31 "With God's help"

One man alive, ankle tendons cleanly cut.

Two men dead, shot through the cervical spine.

Another man alive, ankle tendons cut and an arrow through the thigh. The thigh had begun to swell, much like the Amalekite who suffered from the porcupine quill.

The fifth man, the messenger, was found farther down the mountain. He'd been dragged or crawled quite a ways. His clothes and skin were torn as if by wild animals. Hyenas, maybe. A leopard. Wolves. The dead man's eyes were open, fixed in horror.

The silver-streaked boy was gone.

Now they had only eleven men and a slave to transport the melekh's armorer to the waiting ship.

CHAPTER THIRTY-SIX

Shira saw Baka from the tower. It could only be Baka. A lone donkey with some tattered red yarn where a halter should be. Shira had been going up to the tower for several hours per day, watching toward the south and west.

Disregarding any decorum, she descended the ladder rapidly, sending her bodyguard below tripping over his own feet in his haste to avert his gaze. While the other bodyguard on the tower scrambled to follow, Shira raced toward the gate, not even bothering to respond to the gate guard's shouts of wonder and alarm.

The bodyguards caught up to her, but Baka had increased her gait to a choppy lope at the sight of the fortress. Home. Food. Fresh water. Sweet dates. Shade for resting. Ear scratches. Kind words.

One of the bodyguards held up his hands, and Baka slowed to a walk, then a stop. He took her muzzle, inspecting her, but Shira went to Baka's neck, quickly finding the braided-in scroll case. Baka butted her head against Shira, scratching her itchy head. Shira worked with her fingers, but one of the bodyguards drew his short sword and cut it loose. Once again Shira worked her fingers, this time over the oiled leather, until the parchment unrolled. Shira read the words and looked up.

"Take this straight to Captain Avidan. Nachshon is at Har Karkom."

This time, her bodyguard had no trouble pointing his feet in the right direction.

An hour later, Baka was refreshed with clear water, resting comfortably in her shaded stall, when Shira poured a sweet mash of barley and dates into her trough.

Home. Water. Food. Shade. Rest. And the fine lavender and mint fly repellent ointment like the boy wore. *L'bayitah, Baka, l'bayitah*. She loved those words. Home.

Oddly, Shira's bodyguards who saw Baka approach the outer gate to Tamar later reported strange shadows flitting above her, like night hawks. The shadows were long and narrow, almost like serpents, they said, with wings and maybe with curved tails like scorpions. Shira never spoke of it.

CHAPTER THIRTY-SEVEN

"Go after him," said the Kitti to the Edomites. "Run him down before he reaches Borot Lotz. It's the closest outpost, but he's on foot. You can find him before he reaches it. Capture him or kill him if you must. We'll prepare here to travel as soon as you return with him."

Everyone except Nachshon's guards, Shua, the Kitti, and Sar Hadad scrambled down the wadi to catch and bring up their mounts. The problem though, was that some of the horses were lame, unable to walk up the game path out of the wadi. After examining their feet, the problem was evident: they'd been quicked in one hoof. They could move only slowly, and they would be doing a lot of standing on three legs for the next couple of days. It took an extra twenty minutes to sort the ones who were sound from those who were lame.

Those who could find a sound horse led it up and out of the wadi. The Edomites quickly bridled their mounts and threw the saddle-cloths across their backs. After tightening the girths and strapping on quiver and bow, they swung up onto the saddle-cloths. The second Edomite to mount his horse screamed. The horse reared and bucked, dumping the rider to the ground.

A third Edomite who was about to mount paused, sensing some new calamity had befallen them. The fallen rider grabbed at the tender part of his thigh, moaning, "The porcupine quills. Check the saddle-cloths for the quills. He's hidden quills in the saddle-cloths. He poisoned them..."

The rider who was already mounted leaped back down and felt cautiously along the back of his horse for a quill concealed between the layers of cloth. The rest of the riders did the same. Two of them found broken pieces of quills worked cunningly between the layers of cloth, aimed up. Only after uncinching the cloths and casting them aside did they mount and ride away.

CHAPTER THIRTY-EIGHT

The Edomite who'd been pierced with the poison quill looked around to locate his horse, but even as he gained his feet, everyone knew he was finished. A day. Two days. Three at the most. The silver-haired boy's poison was lethal.

Sar Hadad and the Kitti looked at one another.

"Ever since that desert wolf arrived," said Sar Hadad, "we've gone from a perfect execution of our plan to half our men and horses. I suspect he even poisoned our food."

"Not likely," said the Kitti. "You're seeing shadows again. He hasn't gone near our food."

"Not while we were awake," snapped Sar Hadad.

"You! Slave!" barked the Kitti.

Shua stood from working with the small fire he'd kindled, but it had gone out during the search for the night watch. "Adoni," he answered.

"Did that boy ever go near the food supply?"

"No, my lord. Not that I saw. Last night he only drew water for me and poured for the porridge..." Shua stopped, widening his eyes.

Sar Hadad's face paled.

"It's in your head," said the Kitti. "We'd have already fallen ill."

"I heard wolves howling in the night. We should go now," said Sar Hadad. "Forget the escort. Just find the sound horses, take Nachshon and the guards, and ride for Scorpions' Ascent. Let the guards kill the tax collectors while you and I take Nachshon and ride over. By the time word reaches the fortress, we'll be on the other side. And by the time they muster troops to pursue us, we'll be to the seaport."

The Kitti didn't respond immediately.

"The fortress wouldn't have to muster troops," said Shua. "Your spy said they use messenger rock doves. The fortress keeps messenger doves from Be-er Sheva, Etzion-Geber, and Yerushalayim."

"I knew that," said Sar Hadad shaking his head at himself. "I knew that. We'll need all the men to create enough distraction. It takes more travelers to pull in the extra guards from the trail steps. They only come in to supervise a large tax collection or if there are men of fighting age on horseback."

The Kitti gazed silently toward the burning orange sun rising over the wilderness of Paran and the mountain of the moon god. The mountain was still bathed in gray morning mist. Faded. Blurry.

"Shall we risk riding through the outposts south of the Scorpions? Try to avoid the Akkrabim so we can't be trapped?" asked Sar Hadad.

"It's your country," snapped the Kitti. "You said it would be like walking across a field of vipers to make it through there without being recognized. By now, they are all looking for Nachshon and a band of armed men on horseback. You tell me, which is worse, being trapped by the Scorpions or shot at from every hill between here and The Great Sea?"

"I was raised in Egypt," Sar Hadad snapped back. "I depend upon my spies here among my Edomite people. I've spent more time in Kittim than here. My son is practically a Kitti. Now my best desert scouts are dead."

"We cannot fail," the Kitti warned Sar Hadad. "My warriors are expecting the forges to fire soon for their new iron swords and spears. You have shipbuilders building the vessels to carry an army and to siphon the trade wealth of the sons of Nevaiot. Yavan threatens us to the east. Only weapons and trade will unify the clans of Latium. Romulus must rise."

"We will not fail," said Sar Hadad. "I've spent my life planning this day. My son and I will conquer and re-take our kingdom." Sar Hadad looked toward the hut where Nachshon was held. "I will kill that boy before I allow him back in the hands of Melekh Shlomo. Let my Edomite warriors capture the little wolf. If they don't kill him, then I will cut him in pieces before his father's very eyes. And I will kidnap Nachshon's sons one by one and cut them in pieces until he divulges every secret of the fire."

Sar Hadad looked toward his soldier, who was trying vainly to grab his horse's reins. The horse kept shying away, somehow sensing the poison of man and beast working inside him.

The Kitti smiled a little. "A quick death saves time and trouble, but you have a point." He looked at Shua. "Finish preparing breakfast, slave. Then go through the rest of the saddle cloths and search for more of the poison quills. After we eat, we'll go down to the wadi and bring up the rest of the sound horses. No need to hide them now. We'll ride as soon as the men return." He looked back at Sar Hadad. "With or without the wolf cub."

CHAPTER THIRTY-NINE

Tzakhi stopped at the camp where he'd hidden Baka's pack and The Levite's sword. He'd kept one of the Amalekites' swords and all their water-skins along with extra arrows. He'd retrieved his own bow, quiver, and the rest of the poisoned arrows.

He'd had a choice: take one of the swift horses and ride, or take flight on foot. If he'd taken a horse, he'd have risked the other horses whinnying after it and alerting the camp with the sound of hooves on the plateau. He'd have riders after him within ten minutes. On foot, he'd have most of the night and the advantage of leaving little sign.

If he could evade, perhaps they'd give up the chase after a day and choose a hasty flight over the Scorpions' Ascent. The soldiers of the Akkrabim would trap them.

Whatever the desert would give, Tzakhi needed. Tonight, the full moon had smiled on Tzakhi. His arrows had been true. The Edomites worshiped the moon god at the Sin mountain, but like Tzakhi's so-called magic, there was no god on that mountain. There was only one God, and acknowledging this meant appreciating the qualities of His creation. Tzakhi knew how HaShem designed the desert...its seasons, its inhabitants, and like HaShem Himself, its utter disregard for the plans of human beings.

The closest outpost was located at the cisterns of Borot Lotz. Tzakhi prayed that riders wouldn't follow him, but he'd had to leave sound horses. He'd had only enough time to quick some of them in a single hoof during his water deliveries. Some had maybe already healed. Riders could overtake him once they sorted through and found the sound horses.

The cold disregard of the desert furnace might be overruled if HaShem did shine His face on him, so Tzakhi prayed more than once even after praying the morning Shema. The weaving night cloud shadows didn't bother him. In fact, they seemed to know where he was going and flew ahead on the trail when it grew faint in the gloom so he didn't wander.

It made no sense to go exactly where the man-stealers expected him to go, but there was nowhere else he could go within a day's walking distance. If the riders left at dawn, they'd run him down a few hours' walk from Borot Lotz. The cliffs would slow him more than they would horses.

Any other destination would demand more energy than he could muster with the scraps of food he'd taken from the guards.

Any other destination, like Karka, risked missing soldiers who might come to the rescue.

Any other destination risked him not knowing if the band would ride toward Scorpions' Ascent with Abba.

Sometimes a bad choice is the only choice.

CHAPTER FORTY

Tzakhi was tired. His feet were on fire as if he wore no sandals at all, and it was still a few hours away from noon. He had a skin of water, but he'd drawn liberally from the other waterskin because the desert sapped moisture without one realizing it until it was too late. He couldn't afford to stop and make a shade to rest. Each step took a concentrated, heavy effort.

He knew riders were close. There was no defensive position he could take that offered real concealment or protection of his flank. If he stood and drew his bow, the riders would simply split up and encircle him, willing to lose a horse or rider, knowing he'd be unable to re-string an arrow before he was shot himself. Besides, more often than not, their formed leather breastplates would deflect a less-than-perfect arrowshot.

With each passing minute, he looked over his shoulder, causing himself to fall a few times when he didn't see a rock or too-soft sand. Finally, he saw a rider top a rise far behind him. Another. Another. Six in all.

He'd stuck to the trail to Borot Lotz and Makhtesh Ramon, hoping to encounter other travelers who might help or even Captain Avidan. Had he veered off the trail, he might have evaded, but he'd lose the opportunity to find help that might save Abba before he disappeared into Egypt or across the Scorpions' Ascent to a waiting ship. Even if Avidan were coming, it was too late now. What did Tzakhi have left but a short exchange of arrows? The riders would see him, spread out, encircle him, and kill him.

Better to die trying than to die not trying.

They were moving fast, taking advantage of the cooler morning temperature. If Tzakhi ran off the trail, they'd see him or track the foot-dimples in the sand. Their vantage point from horseback was better than his. They, too, knew they were close. Each rider carefully scanned the trail for his sign. The shadows stopped moving, creating odd patches of faint shade on the sand he could only ever catch from the corner of his eye. Were they marking the end of his trail?

Quickly, Tzakhi assessed the area. An acacia tree. It was little cover, but it was something. There was a small field of broken rocks around it. It wouldn't stop a horse, but it would slow them, disrupt a charge. It looked like someone had built a small rock shelter, maybe shepherds, but over time, it had tumbled into a partial wall and a roundish collection of rock. It would force an attacker either to Tzakhi's right or left. Only a moment, but maybe enough time to string an arrow or dodge around the acacia.

First, though, he needed an advantage. Something to help him make the first shot. Maybe two shots before the riders brought their bows or swords to bear. The riders expected him to hide in such an obvious place.

What could the Arava give him now other than a tree and some rocks?

Sand.

Tzakhi removed his turban and buried it with his ration bag, smoothing the sand over them.

He was down to his last full waterskin. May as well gamble it all. He doused himself completely, then covered the waterskin with rocks.

Next, Tzakhi rolled in the sand like a horse scratching its back. Like the wolves rolling in the carrion remains to conceal the predator scent. He rolled until the sand stuck to him all over, even encrusting his hair and forming long, gritty locks. His bow, quiver, and a small reed were all Tzakhi didn't bury. He sometimes used the hollow reed to blow on a small fire to build it. It was a smaller version of the furnace blowers.

Tzakhi found the sandbank closest to the acacia and buried his bow and quiver a little off of the trail. It was all he could do to resist peeking over the top of the dune to see how close the riders were, but if he did, he risked being spotted.

Next, he burrowed into the sand like a snake, but Tzakhi burrowed belly up instead of down. He burrowed between bow and quiver until most of his lower body was concealed. His feet were the biggest problem, so he had to scoop with his hands to make it deeper there. He wriggled and dug, wriggled and dug, until his upper torso was mostly covered. Finally, he closed his eyes and covered his face, holding the small reed in his mouth to breathe.

Tzakhi worked his arms as deeply into the sand as he could, grasped the bow in his right hand, an arrow in his left, working sand over them, too, like a burrowing viper, and waited.

An eternity.

Probably, it was only a few minutes. A few minutes to wonder if the horses would scent him and shy, alerting the riders. A few minutes to wonder how painful it was to die by arrow or sword. A few minutes to wonder if Shira would be okay without Abba. If she would miss Tzakhi. If he would finally see his ima when he crossed over. If Abba Avraham really did escort the righteous dead to Gan Eden. If he would be righteous enough to go there instead of Sheol.

After all, he had now killed men. Melekh David was not permitted to build the Temple because of the blood on his hands. What would his brothers remember of him? Would they think of him sometimes and laugh a little at the memory of their wreck of a sukkah? Oh, and Salmah. Maybe Salmah would understand the danger of silver hair and remain safely with the school of the prophets in Beit El, far away from desert man-stealers. And a strange thought...would the sand go far in his ears?

Then he felt it. A slight concussion in the earth.

Tzakhi waited until the earth was still again. He counted off seconds, knowing horses had good rear vision, or a rider might veer off the trail to look for sign before catching up with the others.

His heart was racing, but this was the end, probably, of Tzakhi's life. All he could do now was try to reduce the number of man-stealers. Maybe Abba could escape if their plan broke down. It would give Captain Avidan time to arrive.

Slowly, like the morning sun over the mountains of Moab, Tzakhi sat up. The riders had been riding in two groups, three abreast on either side of the trail. The riders on each side looked for sign off the trail, and the ones in the middle looked for sign ahead. A slow trot. The middle rider of the rear group sensed something. He stopped his horse and turned just in time to see Tzakhi sit up.

Tzakhi strung the arrow quickly.

Whooooshht! The rider fell, an arrow embedded just above his hardened leather breastplate.

Tzakhi fitted another arrow rapidly and drew the bow just as the other two rear riders reined in their horses and turned to see what had happened. Mistake. Moving targets are harder. They should have ridden forward, right and left, weaving to avoid another arrow. It was too fast, though, for most humans to process.

Whoooooshht! Another arrow. Another hit. The right-hand rider. Shoulder joint. Tzakhi didn't have time to evaluate how good the hit was, though. He had to run faster than he'd ever run in his life. He grabbed his quiver.

As he ran, he strung a third arrow into his bow. The first group had turned to see the source of the disturbance behind them. At first, they just milled together, shouting at one another, and then catching sight of the running sand creature. When Tzakhi reached the acacia, he pulled three more arrows from the quiver and laid them across an elbow of a branch within easy reach.

Four riders...no, five. Riding fast toward him. The second arrow had not disabled the rider.

Tzakhi shifted back and forth under the acacia, denying the riders a clear look. As they charged closer, Tzakhi spied something else. The wolfpack. Some loped along behind the riders, a couple fanned out on either side. Classic wolf hunting formation. They were funneling the unwitting riders like gazelles in a kite. The riders didn't notice the wolves at their heels, but Tzakhi saw the men look up as if trying to see the serpent-scorpions' shadows.

"You're worried about the wrong thing," muttered Tzakhi. "Don't you see them?"

Once the lead rider reached the jagged rocks and slowed, he was within bowshot, and Tzakhi let his arrow fly. It hit the man's shoulder, but it didn't knock him off his horse. The others did exactly what Tzakhi expected they would do. They split up to encircle him.

He let another arrow fly. It glanced off the leather armor. Miss.

A rider flanked him and turned in, but Tzakhi spun and shot. A hard hit. The horse ran away, riderless. The rider was already wearing one arrow Tzakhi had shot from the dune.

This time, an arrow flew by Tzakhi's ear. They must have decided to settle for his silver hair as a trophy and not risk more losses.

Another arrow ricocheted off the acacia. This would be over very soon.

Tzakhi drew another arrow even as one of the riders dismounted and drew his sword, approaching from the front. A sharp shudder went through Tzakhi from an arrow strike on his quiver, but it didn't penetrate. He let another arrow fly. Another skip off the leather armor, but the rider involuntarily yanked his horse's reins, and the horse went down, rolled, and got up, riderless. It, too, galloped away.

The Mother Wolf let the horse go. She did not let the rider. A scream.

Four wolves trailing behind the riders now attacked the closest horseman, dragging him from his horse's back. It was easy because none of the riders was using a saddle-cloth. Another rider swung his bow away from Tzakhi and aimed at the wolves, which was precisely when one of the wolves running in the swing position leaped up and snagged the bowman by his tunic. The arrow launched upward, useless.

The wolf who'd loped along in the other swing position narrowed the vise and snapped at the rider's horse, which made the horse rear. The rider fell backward, landing hard on the rocks. His horse shied away. The rider didn't move, even when the wolf worried at his tunic and ripped at his face. That left the swordsman on foot.

The swordsman, however, was now only two short-swords' distance away. Tzakhi threw down the bow and drew The Levite's sword. He'd practiced with it some on the journey to Har Karkom, learning its balance and weight. It was a good thing. The Edomite was an excellent swordsman. Back and forth their iron flashed.

For the first time, Tzakhi knew he was good. When he used Avidan's cork-stopped sword to practice with the soldiers, he was never sure if they were humoring him because his father was Nachshon, the chief metalworker of royalty. Now he knew.

The Edomite was good, but Tzakhi parried every thrust. And although the Edomite tried to use his bulk to gain advantage with brute force, Tzakhi was faster and lighter on his feet in the sand, and he repeatedly re-gained the advantage. It was the leather armor that blocked his best opportunities.

He could have slipped in a lethal cut, but this was different than shooting the sentries from a distance with his bow. This was very close up. Personal. The man's bigger size was still a threat if Tzakhi scored a lethal cut. Even in death throes, he could grab Tzakhi and counter with a cut of his own.

What finally broke Tzakhi's reluctance was a cut to his forearm that could have ended up below his breastbone if he'd not been faster. This man aimed to kill Tzakhi. So Tzakhi parried one more thrust before he slipped The Levite's blade just under the Edomite's leather armor and thrust upward toward the heart. At the same time, Tzakhi pushed his other forearm close to block, but rather than counter with a last, strong death lunge, the swordsman froze and looked down. His own sword dropped into the pale sand.

It was over quickly after that.

The place was carnage.

Six slain men, some torn. A few wolves worried at the men's ration bags, nosing inside for dried meat and sniffing the dried fruit. For a few, the fallen were food.

Weary with relief, Tzakhi sat down under the tree and drank from a fallen waterskin, spilling some because his hands were shaking. He rinsed the cut on his arm with some of the water. He'd have to pour some water for the wolves, he guessed. They were all panting from the chase. And the kill. He tried not watch or hear what they were doing to the corpses of the fallen men.

CHAPTER FORTY-ONE

When he could stand without his legs shaking, Tzakhi tugged a leather helmet from one of the fallen Edomites and turned it into a watering bowl. He poured for the wolves, who took turns drinking. The Mother Wolf repeatedly sniffed and looked northward. Maybe travelers were coming.

Tzakhi threw the Mother Wolf what was left of the dried meat he had taken from the slain sentries the night before. All the horses had run away but two, and they grazed together at some clumps of greenery in the distance. If Tzakhi could catch one of them, he could make Borot Lotz or even Ramon within a short time. The horses weren't likely to let anything approach them with the wolves lurking around, though.

"Mother Wolf," said Tzakhi. "Thank you. And thank you for your help last night. Please go, but don't go too far. There may be more riders after them."

The dried meat had already been devoured, and the Mother Wolf panted at him for a few moments before turning away. She growled a low growl, which brought the other wolves to heel after her. A couple of them trotted after her with edible treasure still between their teeth.

It took Tzakhi a half hour to catch the reins of both horses. He led them back to the acacia. On one of them, he changed from bridle to halter and formed a lead rope from the reins. The other one he'd ride.

Then, on the horizon, there was the dust of many riders. Many more horses than seven wolves could bring down. And Tzakhi had few arrows left. He looked around, trying to locate the quivers of the fallen men. Or maybe just mount the horse and ride? Where?

CHAPTER FORTY-TWO

There is a dawn at the end of every day. The dazzling sun's light becomes a kinder orange. Its heat subsides as it drops low on the horizon. In the coolness, now able to confront the great light, a human being realizes there are very few minutes left before what must be seen in the light will never again be seen on that day. The realization dawning in those slow minutes cools, a sealed fate, a door closing on the promises one might have made to HaShem or people. No going back.

Although it was nearly noon when the sun was rising to its zenith, the minutes passed for Tzakhi like those of the setting sun, much too fast. Too late to change his mind.

Tzakhi decided to stand on the sandbank to be seen.

It made sense. He could not imagine another detachment of man-stealers unless they had been hiding until an appointed time to come escort the raiding party to the Scorpions' Ascent. It wouldn't have been something they'd have said aloud in the hearing of a vagabond boy wandering the desert with a donkey. A boy who could have passed the information along.

The riders came closer. Tzakhi could tell when they'd spotted him. The lead rider slowed, probably calling to the others. The others paused for several long seconds, then re-formed, pulling bows.

Tzakhi tried to beat the pale sand from his hair and clothes so he wouldn't look like a great sand lizard or madman with a sheid. Once again the riders came toward him, now in a defensive formation, some of the riders protecting the flanks and their rear. Each rider rode in tandem with another who would hold the reins of the rider with partially-drawn bow. This would make the arrows sure, more effective than shots from all the bows without the horses' precise movement. Extra arrows were at the ready on each side of the saddle-cloths.

As they grew closer, Tzakhi pushed away despair. It wasn't Avidan. He didn't recognize the riders. Any of them. He stood his ground, waving.

The riders came no faster. They came cautiously, looking for a trap.

All Tzakhi could do was wait.

Finally, he could see they were wearing the helmet and scale armor of Melekh Shlomo. Tzakhi could have sunk into the sand with relief.

Then, far behind the soldiers, Tzakhi saw another group of riders following. If it was the same number as the detachment approaching him, there would be at least twenty soldiers total plus baggage mules.

The first detachment reached him and slowed, encircling him. Half the bowmen aimed their bows at him, half to the outside. The captain took a look at Tzakhi, then took a much longer look at the slain men lying around. Tzakhi waited for him to look back at him.

"I am Tzakhi ben Nachshon," said Tzakhi. "I have found my father. He is being held at Har Karkom. I escaped the man-stealers and tried to make it to Borot Lotz, but these riders tracked me here." He left it at that. One boy surrounded by several slain men didn't make much sense. He'd have to let the captain process it.

"And what happened to them?" asked the captain. He didn't tell the bowmen to stand down. He was still suspicious of a trap. Admittedly, what Tzakhi was saying didn't look believable.

"I hid in the sand and shot them. Then I defended from the acacia," said Tzakhi.

The captain looked around again, maybe thinking more sand-warriors might pop up out of the dune. "By yourself?"

"Yes, adoni," said Tzakhi. "And a pack of wolves had been tracking them. Some of them tore the riders. Very strange."

"Yes, indeed very strange," said the captain. He looked back to check the progress of the second detachment of riders. He said to his riders, "When Avidan's detachment arrives, check around. I don't believe the boy."

Avidan? Baruch HaShem Adonai.[32]

---

32 Praise the Name of God

CHAPTER FORTY-THREE

When Avidan rode up, Tzakhi resisted the urge to run to him or hug Noa's neck in relief. Avidan squinted at Tzakhi for a moment until he recognized him under his sand suit. "Tzakhi?"

Tzakhi nodded and walked forward. Only then did the bowmen relax, and the first detachment reined their horses in different directions to inspect the battleground.

"You've met Yoachim? The captain from Sela?" asked Avidan.

"Yes, Captain," said Tzakhi. "I don't think he quite believed my story. But maybe if you explain you trained me yourself, it will be more believable."

Avidan looked around at the dead, taking it in, then at the two Egyptian horses Tzakhi had tied to the tree. "These are man-stealers? You did all this yourself?" he asked.

Tzakhi nodded again. "Mostly. Wolves were chasing them, so I can't take all the credit."

At this, Avidan removed his bronze helmet, ran his fingers through sweaty hair, glanced at Captain Yoachim, and replaced the helmet. "I'm not sure I believe it, either. You should explain."

"Could I explain as we ride?" asked Tzakhi. "I know where Abba is. If you don't believe this, then you might have trouble believing what I did back at their camp. And they'll be expecting this squad to have captured me and to return soon. I don't want them to spook and ride to Egypt when they don't return."

Avidan nodded this time, and Captain Yoachim called in his soldiers. "Leave the man-stealers to the hyenas, vultures, and jackals."

Tzakhi mounted one captured horse and led the other. Both captains rode in front with him so they could listen to his story.

"It's Sar Hadad and a man from Kittim who hold Abba at Har Karkom," said Tzakhi. "If one of you leads me on one of the Edomites' horses and rides the other, maybe they'll think it's their men and they've captured me. They may not notice the other horses as much. Like their own, you are riding chestnuts and bays. I can ride as if my hands are tied. We can get close until they see you're wearing scale instead of leather armor. By the time they mount up...and that will be a problem...we'll be upon them. The second detachment could cut off retreat toward the south and approach from there."

"If so," said Captain Yoachim, "it will trap them and force them into Egypt."

"It would only be a last resort," said Tzakhi, "or they would have already traveled that way. Pharaoh doesn't know what Sar Hadad has done. If they did ride into Egypt, they'd turn toward the coast. They're trying to go to Kittim, not Egypt. And only two of them can ride fast. Unless they ride one of the mules."

"And why will it be a problem for them to mount up? Why can only two ride?" asked Captain Avidan.

"I quicked their horses and a mule," said Tzakhi. "The riders who chased me were riding the sound ones. There's only a couple of sound horses left in their herd."

"So they'll stand and fight," said Captain Yoachim.

"Yes, adoni, probably," said Tzakhi. "But there's only six of them left, a Hebrew slave, and Abba. Good fighters, I'm sure, but now they're outnumbered."

"Why do you say, 'only six of them left'?" asked Avidan. "How many did they start with?"

"I'm not sure how many were in the raiding party," said Tzakhi. "Some of them rode toward Ashur to deceive the trackers. There were twenty men with their horses and two baggage mules camped at Har Karkom guarding Abba."

Captain Yoachim said, "There are six men dead back there. What happened to the other seven?"

How to tell them? Tzakhi looked up, thinking the shadow-clouds might move across the sky, showing the captains not everything in this part of the Arava was so straightforward. Nothing. No sign of the wolves, either. The horse soldiers had seen the torn corpses. Hopefully, they didn't think he did it. Those definitely weren't sword or arrow wounds.

Tzakhi took the opportunity to collect himself by drinking water from a waterskin. When he tied off the spout and dropped the waterskin back along the horse's withers, he wiped wet sand from his mouth. Both captains waited.

"One went mad when a sandstorm blinded him. The Kitti cut his throat."

"One was bitten by a scorpion."

"One stepped on a porcupine quill coated in viper venom. Both had infected wounds. The Kitti killed them, too."

"Two were shot with arrows on the night watch. Two others had their ankle tendons cut, and one of them was shot with a venomous arrow as well."

"Some may have sat on saddle cloths with venomous quills hidden inside."

"Another one...a pack of wolves chased him down the mountain. He's dead."

Captain Avidan and Captain Yoachim looked at one another. They rode in silence for a while. Finally, Captain Yoachim broke the silence. "You're not going to tell me wolves killed all those men back there, are you?"

Tzakhi said, "No, Captain. I buried myself in the sandbank, and after they rode over, I shot two of them from behind. After that, I took cover behind the acacia and used the fallen wall to help cover my flanks. When they rushed me and tried to surround me, the wolves closed in. It distracted them enough for me to make some shots. While I fought one of the Edomites with a sword, the wolves finished the fallen riders, and well...you saw. The younger males were a little more aggressive."

"And they didn't attack you?" inquired Avidan.

"No, Captain."

"Nu?³³ Why not?"

Tzakhi sighed, wondering if he dared. The story was so fantastic already, maybe it didn't matter. He said, "It's my wolfpack from Ein Tzin. My brother Salmah showed me how to talk to them. They've been following me the entire journey. I feed them, and they...help."

"You talk to them?" asked Yoachim, maybe with less disbelief than Tzakhi expected.

"I do. When I need them, I call them on my shofar. I can make it sound like a wolf-howl. I talk to them, but it's more like we just understand one another. I don't know when Salmah found them, but they connect with us somehow."

---

33 So?

"So if you blew your shofar right now," said Captain Yoachim, "They would come attack us?"

"Not at first," said Tzakhi. "They follow and watch. They help me the way wolves hunt. There's a long time of following, waiting, and then they form up and attack. Well, maybe not the Amalekite night watchman at Karkom. They just surrounded him, and he ran. There wasn't much of a scream, so I guess they went for his throat first."

"Are they following us now?" asked Avidan.

"I don't know," said Tzakhi. "I asked the Mother Wolf...she's the leader...to please take them away. They were scaring the horses. But you can watch your horses, and they'll tell you if they catch the scent. Some of the wolves left with bloody muzzles. But I don't think they'll come if I don't call them."

Captain Avidan reined in his horse, which brought both detachments to a halt. He scanned the horizon, maybe looking for the wolves. Seeing nothing, he motioned the soldiers in. "Everybody drink. Check your equipment. I'll tell you our plan, then Tzakhi will describe the terrain to you. After that, we ride hard."

CHAPTER FORTY-FOUR

Avidan's detachment crested the plateau in a sudden gallop. Sar-Hadad spotted them first. He yelled toward the huts, which brought the guards out with swords drawn. The Kitti emerged from the sleeping hut and just stood for several moments, sizing up the enemy, looking different directions.

Tzakhi slipped the loose bonds from his hands. Shua was at the lookout as Tzakhi had asked him. And just as Tzakhi had asked, Shua failed to sound the alarm of the approaching cavalry. Tzakhi galloped his horse toward Shua, stopped between him and the fighting, and slid from the horse's back. He scanned the camp and pulled The Levite's sword from under his tunic.

Tzakhi beckoned to Shua. "Come with me," he shouted. "Away from the battle."

Shua first ran, then slowed to walk, perhaps thinking the soldiers might misunderstand it as an attack on Tzakhi. Just then, Tzakhi saw Matukah watching alertly. Some of the quicked horses had found their way up the wadi, perhaps following their companions who were sound. The remaining sound horses and mule stood tied, close to the huts, already kitted for a fast escape.

Tzakhi had done the shallowest of scraping on the lame ones' feet so they would not be in pain as long as they stood still or walked in the sand. Some of them had already healed enough to walk slowly about the camp.

"I want to catch my donkey," Tzakhi said to Shua. "Come with me." He trotted toward Matukah, who scented him and broke into a lope toward him. For the first time ever, Tzakhi could see her sides heaving, attempting to bray, yet no sound emerged.

"I made sure she was fed and watered," said Shua. "I tried not to overload her with the water skins."

"Thank you," said Tzakhi. He handed Shua the reins to his horse.

When they met, Tzakhi wrapped his arms around Matukah's dark neck and rubbed her mane before he turned to check the combat. Avidan had told him to stay away from the fighting just in case the wolves didn't know the difference between an Edomite and an Israelite soldier.

On the other side of the camp, Avidan's elite detachment engaged the remaining guards. Two Israelite soldiers had already positioned themselves between the guards and Abba, who had finally emerged from his prison hut. His hands were bound, and his red hair and beard had grown longer than Tzakhi had ever seen.

Abba's Edomite guards were trying to fight backward toward their horses using short swords. The Kitti and Sar Hadad fought as well. Sar Hadad swung an Egyptian-style curved sword, and he broke from the group. He reached his mount, and rather than turn the horse north, he turned west toward the mountain. The Kitti also swung aboard his horse, but he turned north.

Sar Hadad galloped his mare up to the table of the mountain peak, turning her toward Egypt. It would be safety for him, at least long enough to plead his case before Pharaoh or to board a ship to Kittim, Yavan, or even Tarshish. Avidan galloped after him, but the captain's Hittite Noa was no match for Sar Hadad's fleet Egyptian mare. Sar Hadad would escape.

The Egyptian border was not far, and Captain Avidan would not breach it. The pharaoh was touchy about Melekh Shlomo's military outposts so close to the border. This whole ordeal was about to end in a lost horse race.

Then something else happened. The moment Sar Hadad's horse gained the level of the plateau, a strange cloud began forming around the mountain. It was strange because it wasn't part of a storm cloud. Instead, it started as a white mist atop one of the peaks, grew, swirled, thickened, and began cracking lightning and rumbling, all within a minute.

Echoes multiplied as thunder rolled and smashed down through the wadis and up against the heights. It was as if the sounds became substance, charring and splitting rocks with white, glowing heat. The storm's sounds were super-heated like the hottest wind-fired furnace on Givat Chatzeva.

The sounds reminded Tzakhi of the whoosh of a palm frond when swung quickly, yet to his ears, the whooshing was words he'd read in the Torah scrolls. He could understand all the rushing sound-words even though the echoes made them as many as the stars of the sky. The lightning instantly smelted sand into spots of splashing liquid, then into glass like green-black obsidian.

Tzakhi backed up several steps, trembling. This was something like the moving serpent-scorpion shadows, something from another realm, but much stronger. Although the storm's strength lay atop him like an invisible weight, it triggered something he read in the Holy Scroll of Shemot[34] with The Levite.

---

34 Exodus

The Levite. The holy man had been with Tzakhi every step of this journey: the tzirah-shadows of whirlwind, the sword, even helping him understand the intrigue guiding Abba's kidnapping. It helped him prepare his weapons for the journey. And knowing the Words of the Holy Scroll sharpened his thinking, giving him the courage to sabotage or kill to make his escape, to save his own life. The first holy scroll of the Torah, Bereishit,[35] said of Shimon and Levi:

> Let my soul not enter into their council;
> Let not my glory be united with their assembly;
> Because in their anger they slew men,
> And in their self-will they lamed oxen.[36]

What did that mean? Now Tzakhi understood. Whether a man or beast must be killed or lamed, let it not be in anger. Let it be justice, not revenge. Let it be for the preservation of life, a fair judgment, not to torture. Only when he truly needed the guidance did the Words sink in. The Levite.

Avidan dispatched the last standing man-stealer, and he and eight riders raced after Sar Hadad. Two riders would not leave Abba's side.

More Words from the second book of the Holy Scroll, Shemot, thundered between Tzakhi's ears. He ran and held up his hands to stop the pursuers. "Don't follow him up there," shouted Tzakhi through the thunder. He wasn't sure if it was the thunder in his head or on the mountain. "You can only go up if you hear

---

35 Genesis
36 Genesis 49:6

the shofar when the cloud is there. If not, if you touch the mountain, you and your horses will die."

Even as the words left his mouth, Sar Hadad's mare reared, pawed at the sky, and fell over backwards. She rolled and regained her feet, leaving Sar Hadad to slowly rise to his knees, and then to stagger to his own feet. The mare raced wildly back toward the camp, lightning striking sparks on the flint around her even as her own hoofs struck sparks.

"Like Bilaam's donkey," muttered Tzakhi. "She knows she'd die with the evil man." The soldiers took a firmer hold on their reins at the sight. Matukah galloped away.

Looking bewildered, Sar Hadad turned himself around, either addled from the fall or unsure what to do next in the deafening roar and exploding light of the whirling desert storm. Great hailstones began to fall, rolling around the plateau like catapult stones. The ones falling on the slope rolled down the terraces, shimmering brightly as if on fire.

Sar Hadad's body convulsed as the hailstones began to hit him, and he ran drunkenly, blindly, finally falling off the plateau onto the terrace below. Unable to orient himself, he remained on his knees, covering his head with his hands. And then a bolt of lightning flashed from the brilliant white cloud. To Tzakhi, it looked like a great jagged arrow shot through Sar Hadad. Dark smoke bloomed around him, and when it receded, nothing was there but a charred garment covered in hailstones.

Sar Hadad's mare slowed to a trot toward Tzakhi and the soldiers who watched. She was looking for the security of a herd. The mare was the beautiful one, a prize from Pharaoh's own stable: dapple gray with exquisitely-turned eartips, long, slender neck, delicately dished face, and large, intelligent black eyes. Her nostrils flared wide from fright and effort, showing pink. She shook her iron-gray mane and held her tail like a battle banner. Her bridle bore the seal of the Egyptian royal stable and its royal colored tassels. Tzakhi had not dared to quick her. She was too regal.

Tzakhi held out his hand, low, beckoning her. The horse and bridle would be something Avidan would need to take to Melekh Shlomo as proof of Sar Hadad's calumny. She slowed to a walk, then planted her front feet abruptly, head held high and eyes rolling at the strange sounds reverberating across the sands.

As the rumbles and flashing lightning receded, Tzakhi eased forward and took her trailing reins. She jumped a bit, but Tzakhi moved with her, putting just a little tension on the reins to steady her. He talked to her in the Egyptian language, and she settled, only dancing a little sideways.

When Tzakhi looked back at the mountain, the storm cloud was disappearing like mist burning off in the morning sun. Never had Tzakhi seen such a storm. It vanished as quickly as it appeared. All that was left was Sar Hadad's tunic and dripping waterfalls and pools of water from the melting hailstones.

Tzakhi turned his head, looking first at Captain Avidan, Shua, and then at the soldiers. They all stared back, silently asking one another the same question: "Did you see the sounds?"

"Back ten steps," commanded Avidan reverently. "Don't turn around until you back ten steps."

Each soldier pulled low on the reins, cueing their mounts to flex their necks downward and tuck their chins. Also bowing their heads, each rider backed his mount slowly. Shua began walking backward. Likewise, Tzakhi didn't want to turn his back to the Presence still lingering on the mountain even with the last thin wisps of evaporating fog. He stepped to the mare's left side, grabbed her mane, and vaulted to her back.

She minced some nervous sideways steps, but Tzakhi took a firm hold on the reins, settled securely, and steadied her barrel with his feet. There was no resistance, so Tzakhi turned her head back toward the mountain and duplicated the soldiers' respectful backward retreat. The mare was well-trained, just suffering the terror of near-immolation. Tzakhi's heart was still pounding, but his mind was somewhat frozen in disbelief.

What had just happened was difficult to believe, but what happened next was a miracle more credible.

So long ago, so long ago.
The beasts of the wilderness,
The beasts of cloud, walked to the storm.
The flying serpent and the stinging scorpion,
The wolf and the calf,
No harm, this storm,
Lie down, no harm.

CHAPTER FORTY-FIVE

The soldier closest to Shua held his sword-tip to Shua's throat. "Wait," cautioned Tzakhi. "He's not Egyptian. He's a Hebrew slave. He gave me flint to cut my bonds last night. He was standing watch, but he didn't alert the man-stealers. His name is Shua."

At this, Avidan reined his horse around to look directly at Shua.

Shua swallowed hard, making his Adam's apple bob, but he didn't run from the drawn sword.

"Sheathe your sword," said the captain to the soldier. Avidan had a strange look on his face. "Shua?"

"Ken, adoni," said the young man, bowing.

"*Ben kama atah?*" asked Avidan in Hebrew.

"*Ani ben esrim v'chamesh,*" answered Shua. *I am twenty-five years old.*

Strangely, Captain Avidan's eyes were shining. Tzakhi had never seen him weep, but now a tear slipped from the corner of his eye. Avidan asked, "*Shua ben...?*"

"*Shua ben Avidan veh-Tirtzah me-Tamar,*" finished Shua, as if he'd never expected to utter those words. "*Aval ha-horim sheli metim.*" *Shua son of Avidan and Tirtzah of Tamar. But my parents are dead.*

"*Lo, b'ni,*" said Avidan. "*Ani lo met. Ani Avidan.*" *No, my son. I am not dead. I am Avidan.*

CHAPTER FORTY-SIX

Shua slumped to his knees. Even Tzakhi leaned his elbows against the gray mare's neck and clutched her mane in disbelief. How could he have not seen the resemblance? Shua's slow, deliberate way of thinking before talking was like Avidan's. Add a beard, and Shua might have been Avidan in his twenties.

Captain Avidan checked their perimeter to make sure they were safe, then he dismounted and went to Shua, who still had not moved. It was a lot to take in. An unnatural cloud. A hailstorm. A man burned to nothing. A father brought to life. A lost son found. A slave freed.

Avidan took Shua in his big arms, and finally Shua broke into great sobs. Tzakhi and the soldiers reined their horses away and left them there.

With some direction from Tzakhi, the soldiers found the two remaining man-stealers Tzakhi had maimed. There would be only one prisoner. The one Tzakhi shot in the thigh with a venomous arrow was already dead, throat cut. That was the work of the Kitti, who eluded them. He was seen galloping in the direction of the Scorpions' Ascent. With him was a lock of Tzakhi's silver hair.

Captain Yoachim's detachment gained the camp's plateau just as Avidan and Shua started walking together toward the camp.

Now that he had Nachshon safely in custody, Avidan declined to chase the Kitti. Yoachim's detachment rode after the fleeing man. One of their riders could stop at Borot Lotz and activate signals and messengers to the Negev outposts, Dimona, Be'er Sheva, and Ashdod to try to intercept the Kitti.

Avidan's horsemen had ridden hard for days, first to escort the malkah of Sheba, then to find Abba, so he ordered them to spend the night and most of the next day in camp resting the horses and themselves. They could refill their waterskins and sharpen their swords before setting their faces toward Tamar the next afternoon when the sun's heat diminished. Tzakhi was sure even the quicked horses and mule would be able to travel by then.

Shua still had plenty of food because Tzakhi had so drastically reduced the number of mouths to feed over the last few days, so he cooked a hot meal of barley and lentil porridge and used the last of the barley flour to bake many flat cakes over a rock. They could take the leftover bread in their ration bags for the trip home.

Shua and Captain Avidan spent much time alone, talking. For all the time Tzakhi remembered Avidan, he'd been a man of few words with those he liked, and nearly none for those he didn't like. Maybe he'd stored them all up for this day.

Tzakhi and the soldiers caught all the horses and returned them to the wadi pen. With this much help, Tzakhi was able to feed and water them all quickly. Matukah refused to leave his side, and she followed him on every trip back and forth from the water cistern to the wadi trough. She nudged him for dates while he checked each horse's hooves, cleaning out some jagged pebbles. He worried about the gray mare, but she seemed only a bit stiff from her fall.

Abba spent a lot of time just walking in the sun, trying to re-gain his strength from being bound in the dark hut for nearly two weeks. Tzakhi's decision to bring him an extra pair of sandals was a clever one. Sar Hadad had hidden Abba's sandals to prevent him from trying to escape, an old Bedouin trick. It was impossible to walk on the desert sand barefoot in the heat of the day.

Abba also spent a couple of hours examining the places where the lightning had burned and broken rocks and turned the sand to molten patches before it turned to dark tubes of glass. It was the charash in him trying to figure out how the heat had transformed the sand. He kept several pieces, probably to crack them open later so he could see the insides.

In the evening, half of the soldiers and Shua retired to their sleeping mats in the guard-hut, and the others scattered to stand watch. Abba, Avidan, and Tzakhi sat around the dying fire. Each offered his part of the story over the last days.

Fortunately, other than seeing his bodyguards killed, Abba had been treated fairly well. Avidan's journey had been a lot of hard riding. It was Tzakhi's story that wove them together.

Tzakhi told his part of the story while Avidan and Abba listened. He thought carefully before saying the words aloud, afraid Abba would think him a strange boy like Salmah. The part about the wolves had something to do with Tzakhi's silver hair, so there was no way around it. He told them briefly of the Kitti's strange oracle from Latium.

Abba said, "The man's story is similar to the story of Ya'akov and Esav. They had a sibling rivalry resulting in two nations: Israel and Edom. Although Esav purposed to kill his brother Ya'akov, he never did. But this story sounds like the Romulus brother kills the Remus brother."

Tzakhi said, "The leader told me, 'I thought I found the world's greatest armorer, but I found the father of Remus from the prophecy. Should I kill you now and return your silver head to

Latium, or should I carry you there alive for the barbarians to give you a ceremonial death and celebrate the victory when Romulus will rise?'"

Abba asked, "He thought you had an ancestor from Kittim?"

"He thought so because of the oracle. And I think maybe he is right. Ima used to sing a song to Salmah and me. She made us learn it. *So long ago, so long ago...* In his head, Tzakhi worked through the lullaby's verses, placing the words of the Kitti alongside them before speaking them into the night fire.

He continued, "The Kitti told me some of the prophecy while they had me tied up. It says the twins named Romulus and Remus will be fathered by Mars, their war god. Their mother will be from someplace in Latium called Alba Longa. 'Long White.' Maybe that's why the boy's hair turns white in the oracle. I suppose it's a place in Kittim. The twins' grandfather will be killed by a competitor, and they will be saved by a river god when they are left to die. They will be raised by wolves afterward...I'm not too sure about this part...the Kitti explained the details while he was eating, and he wasn't well-mannered. They'd tied me up, too, and I was mostly thinking about how to escape, not about idol-worshipers' stories."

"Understood," said Avidan, "but try to remember. It might help us understand his thinking."

Tzakhi went on, "He said after the twins are grown, they will fight over something, and Romulus will kill Remus. In Ima's song, though, there is a son of the killed twin who escapes, though, a green-eyed boy whose long hair turns silver like a wolf's."

Avidan asked, "Why like a wolf?"

"Ima's song says the son will escape back to the wolves who raised him, and the wolves will help him, like the wolves of the Tzin helped me," said Tzakhi. "Maybe they still consider him family. Wolves are like that. They care for the pack. Talk to one another. Dance..." he stopped.

Avidan and Abba didn't need to hear him talk more about the ghost-wolves dancing to Salmah's flute or making a boy's hair turn to frost. They definitely didn't need to hear he'd seen the shadows of the tzirah. Let them think the man-stealers were evil men driven mad by the wilderness.

"What happens then?" asked Nachshon.

"That's where the Kitti prophecy and ima's song confused me. When I understood the prophecy was about two sets of twins that will be born, but her song was mostly from long ago, it made more sense. The twins born long ago in Ima's song are a prophecy of twins who haven't yet been born. They will establish a kingdom when they're born. Sar Hadad learned of the prophecy from the Kittim, and he believes he can use it to take his kingdom back... and I think he wants to have their kingdom, too."

"Why did he think you were part of their prophecy?" prompted Avidan.

Tzakhi answered, "In Ima's song, the long-ago boy who escaped to the wolves grew, had a family, and there was some kind of great fire, and they sailed to Egypt. His daughter married a Benjamite in Egypt, and in time, they became enslaved to Pharaoh with the Israelites. Their babies were thrown into the water. They left Egypt along with the Israelites and went to Canaan."

"That's Israelite history. The Kitti thought you descended from such a union?" asked Abba.

"I don't think he knows that part, Abba. It was just my hair. Remember, one of the twins, Romulus, will kill the other one, Remus. That's the end of the story for the Kitti. But in Ima's song, a son escaped back to the wolves. Then the hair of the boy turns white, there's some great fire, and they sail to Egypt where they are taken in by the Israelite tribe of Benjamin. I'm confused because the song and the oracle are so many years apart. Ima's song ends in the wilderness journey from Egypt. The Kitti's Latium oracle hasn't even happened yet. The Kitti thought he could take my head back to Latium, and it would inspire the tribes to organize. They would see that the Remus twin will be defeated and Romulus' empire will rise. It would prove their oracle is true. I am some kind of omen of their good fortune. That's what the Kitti told me."

"Many prophecies are not from heaven," said Avidan. "They are speculations that drive people to fulfill them. Suggestions shrouded in mystery to give them credence."

Abba asked, "Is that all he said?"

"Only that later, even after Romulus kills Remus, there's one more key that must unlock their great kingdom, something about the Perat River and a swamp or mud or something. He stopped there."

Avidan gazed into the fire for a while, and so did Abba. When Tzakhi felt eyes on him, he looked up, and Abba was staring at him as if for the first time. "Are you sure your ima's song ended there?" he asked.

"*Lo*," said Tzakhi. "There was something else, but it's hard to remember. It was different. Ima didn't always sing it."

"What do you remember?" asked Abba.

So far ahead, so far ahead,
brothers rise, brothers of blood,
brothers dyed red...

Tzakhi couldn't pull more from his memory. "That's all I can remember, but Sar Hadad and the Kitti wanted to take me alive to Latium and sacrifice me to their gods. It would inspire the leaders to link their clans, go on a quest for some special water from the

Perat River, and build their kingdom. The sacrifice of a "white long-hair son" would be proof that Latium would rise."

"And Edom," said Abba.

"And Edom," agreed Tzakhi. "I think I want Shira to cut my hair when we get home."

Both men chuckled a little.

"It's quite a prophecy and quite a song," said Avidan. "But it is a prophecy of idol-worshipers, and kingdoms take hundreds of years to form, to rise, and to fall. Look how many hundreds of years have passed since our ancestors left Egypt."

Abba nodded. "Hundreds."

"Yet," Avidan added, "this strange battle between you and the man-stealers took place at Har Karkom. It's not really one mountain, but twin peaks."

No one responded.

All three of them stared at the fire silently for several more minutes. Avidan broke the silence, "All this will require a private conversation with B'nayahu, the commander of Melekh Shlomo's army. I'll ride to Yerushalayim before the Feast of Sukkot and speak with him. Tzakhi, until I hear from B'nayahu, I'm giving you Sar Hadad's mare to care for, and I'm putting you in charge of the Egyptian herd until you leave for Yerushalayim with your abba. By then, the melekh will decide if he wants to confront Pharaoh with the evidence of Hadad's treachery or make it go away quietly so other nations will not get ideas of also kidnapping our metalworkers."

"He'll want this to go away quietly," muttered Abba. "That Egyptian woman..." he let the rest of the sentence trail away, unwilling to voice something perhaps treasonous.

Avidan continued, "I'll tell the Tamar tax administrator to add the provisions for the horses. They are all fine Egyptian mares, so if B'nayahu wants to send them north to Melekh Shlomo's breeding stable, then you and your brothers can caravan them to the Great Feast and turn them over to the melekh's royal stable steward there."

Tzakhi's heart sank a bit. He'd love to have the dappled gray mare. She rode like a dream, and he'd tried to calculate how long he could pay for her quality fodder out of his caravan earnings. She wasn't his, though. No fourteen-year-old boy owned a fine Egyptian mare unless he were royalty.

The captain must have sensed his disappointment. "But I'll recommend that you be awarded Hadad's mare as a reward for recovering the melekh's charash. The melekh would certainly do it for anyone else. You should be no different."

CHAPTER FORTY-SEVEN

The next afternoon, the horses were caught, bridled, and packed for the trip home to Tamar. Shua and Tzakhi packed as much fodder and as many waterskins as they could onto the baggage mules. Tzakhi placed a light burden of waterskins on Matukah even though he didn't bother to attach a lead rope to her halter. Matukah followed him like a dog already. She'd been so glad to see him after the fight at Karkom that she'd sometimes just lean against him or rub her head against him while he worked around the camp.

Their band set off in formation, half the soldiers ahead of Abba, Tzakhi, and Avidan, and half behind them, followed by Shua and another soldier leading pack mules and the man-stealers' horses.

This gave Abba, Tzakhi, and the captain more time to talk.

Abba said, "Sar Hadad has watched our mining camps through spies all his adult life. I tried to find them and send them away, but Hadad knew almost as much about the mines as the king. Including how many sons I have."

Tzakhi turned that over, but he didn't understand what Abba was saying.

Abba continued, "He would never kill a son of Nachshon who worked the mines. He would use them. But a son without the knowledge would be leverage for him. Like Tzakhi, a symbolic sacrifice to build support for his aims. A hostage in return for secrets of the fire."

"I will be safe, Abba," said Tzakhi. "Sar Hadad is...emmm...gone."

"But the Kitti knows. He's the one who is building a coalition army from the tribes in Latium," said Abba. "He and Hadad were of one mind. And Hadad has a son there. Genuvat."

Tzakhi said, "Melekh Shlomo's soldiers at every outpost will be told to watch for travelers from Kittim. I am always among soldiers. It will be too difficult for them to track my movements without being detected themselves."

"It's not you I'm worried about. They know about Salmah. Is a school of the prophets stronger than the prophecy of Latium?"

"So Salmah may be in danger," said Tzakhi.

"Maybe. Probably not now, but he's become a target much easier than you. The people of Yavan and Kittim are very superstitious. They'll be leery of laying hands on you again if they learn of everything that happened, especially with the wolves."

The journey home to Tamar was mostly quiet afterward. They traveled first east to the Arava highway, then turned north at the Einot springs onto the main highway from Eilat to Tamar. At the springs, Abba showed them where his bodyguards were attacked while they watered horses on the way to Timna. Although the corpses had been returned to Tamar by the shepherds, the soldiers stacked a memorial rock where each of Abba's bodyguards fell. The journey from there felt more normal to Tzakhi. No wolves. No whirlwinds. No hailstorms or lightning-arrows.

No flying shadows.

Tzakhi had seen the shadows a final time the afternoon when they set out from Har Karkom. The shadows flew north, toward Scorpions' Ascent. Tzakhi could only hope they would help Captain Yoachim find the Kitti.

CHAPTER FORTY-EIGHT

From afar, Tzakhi could see the flurry of activity at Tamar when their party was spotted. Abba and Avidan rode at the head of the detachment, and Tzakhi had retreated to the rear with Shua, leading the mules and Egyptian horses. From experience, Tzakhi knew the soldiers would be taking up defensive positions on the towers, walls, and at the gates while the soldier with the best eyesight called out what he could see as they approached.

From the outermost tents surrounding Tamar, one boy or many might ride their donkeys to the fortress to give specifics of the arrival. It depended upon the travelers' importance, and it was an excuse to race. Often a donkey arrived riderless from the pushing and pulling that went on. One of the horse-soldiers sounded his shofar, announcing the peaceful approach of Avidan's detachment.

Today, though, the shofar was unnecessary. They were recognized by those in the tents on the outskirts of Tamar, and the joyful ululations began long before they arrived at the water trough of Tamar to sort out the stock. Boys scrambled aboard their donkeys to be the first to report Avidan and Nachshon's arrival to the tower soldier.

Soon they were surrounded by women singing victory songs and playing timbrels, and boys played small drums. The younger boys trotted alongside the horses, touching the riders' long leather shin armor. The men greeted the soldiers they knew, and all greeted Nachshon and Captain Avidan. All of it excited the horses, who flexed their necks, pricked their ears, and stepped lightly even though weary from two weeks of hard travel.

"Remember it?" Tzakhi asked Shua.

Shua smiled and shook his head. "Not really. I don't remember there being this many people. Not nearly as many tents, and the fortress has been built upon, I think."

"*Mah kara?*" shouted the men at them. *What happened?*

Avidan pointed toward the fortress, indicating he'd tell the story there. Tzakhi wondered how much he'd tell.

Just as Abba reined his horse toward the water trough, Shira burst through the crowd. Abba dropped from his mount and hugged her, kissed her cheeks, and hugged her again. It was the first time Tzakhi had seen them demonstrate any affection in public. Shira buried her face in Abba's chest, and Tzakhi could see her back heaving as she wept. Abba laid his cheek atop hers, mouthing something Tzakhi could not hear. He looked away, feeling as though it was something very private.

Tzakhi was glad, though. He loved them both, and he had always worried that Abba was too busy to give her the affection she needed. This desert was hard on everyone, but especially on women. There was something about witnessing Abba and Shira's grateful embrace that made Tzakhi ache with the memory of his ima.

By the time all the riders filled the great pen around the long water trough, the area was filled with people singing, smiling, drumming, jingling timbrels. Horses and donkeys whinnied and brayed, adding to the commotion. Baka brayed loudly at Matukah, who didn't bray back, but they met and rubbed their muzzles on one another's shoulders, and Baka nibbled happy scratches on Matukah's back.

Tzakhi and Shua dismounted along with the soldiers. One of the soldiers untied the captive Edomite from his horse and dragged him toward the shade of the pen wall. He motioned to a foot soldier to guard him. Tzakhi wondered if he'd ever walk again.

People looked at the Edomite and Shua curiously. The Edomite was clearly a captive. Shua had the short haircut and clothes of an Egyptian, so his story was yet to be told. Tzakhi and Shua started untying the captured horses and turning them toward the trough to drink, but Avidan beckoned to the royal stable grooms and foot soldiers to come take over the job.

Wearily, they assembled with the horse soldiers on the small hill under the great jujube tree while Abba and Avidan prepared to speak. Elad, Tzakhi's oldest brother, broke through the crowd and paused, looking Abba up and down. Abba held open his arms, and they embraced, exchanging cheek kisses. Elad must have been working on Givat Chatzeva when he was summoned. He still wore his leather spark apron and headcover.

The crowd had pressed around, and they offered words of comfort to Abba and Elad at their reunion. The royal steward smiled and turned to Avidan. "Speak, please," he said. "We sing praises of HaShem, the Metzaveh[37] of armies. Tell us the story of victory."

Captain Avidan was a man of few words, but today his mouth was filled with them. "The Arava is a vast wilderness," said Avidan. "Yet, to those who make this their home, it is small. Many people pass through here. I took Tamar as a permanent post for two reasons. One, I love the desert. Melekh David found refuge here.

---

37 Commander

Many of his tehillim were composed in the Arava. It is a place to love or hate. Nothing in between."

Many heads nodded, and there was a low rumble of approval. A few of the conscripted soldiers looked abashed.

"Two, I lost my wife Tirtzah here, may her memory be for blessing. My son was lost and sold into slavery while I was fighting with Melekh David in the Long Campaign. I knew many people pass through here, and if I could search the caravans, maybe one day I would find him and redeem him," said Avidan.

Tzakhi was envious of how boldly Avidan spoke. His voice rang through the crowd with confidence, just as he gave orders to his soldiers.

"And now, Tzakhi has found his father Nachshon, and with the help of HaShem, he redeemed his father from the snare of the enemy. Tzakhi also found my son, Shua, and redeemed him from the bonds of an evil man."

A gasp swept across the crowd.

Avidan beckoned Tzakhi and Shua forward.

They looked at one another, both embarrassed. "*Bo-u!*" insisted Avidan, and the crowd and soldiers encouraged them to come forward.

Together Tzakhi and Shua stepped out of the knot of dusty, weary soldiers.

"Tonight around the fire," said Avidan, "Nachshon and I will tell the story of the Arava, a story to tell alongside those of Melekh David. It is a story of donkeys, of serpents, of scorpions, of wolves, and a miraculous killing desert storm."

This quieted the crowd.

"I have heard the unkind things said of Tzakhi because of his silver hair," said Avidan. "But he is a true son of Nachshon, fearless, a master of desert-craft. HaShem chooses our hair color, not us. Tzakhi is a craftsman like his abba, but the desert has trained and refined him in its own fires according to HaShem's will."

"Amein," shouted The Levite.

"Amein," murmured the crowd.

Captain Avidan glared a little as he looked around, perhaps letting his gaze rest upon specific ones who'd joked about Tzakhi's hair. Ben-Shimi looked down. The captain continued, "To make sport of someone's body, a creation of HaShem, is to say HaShem does not know how to form a human being for His purposes. Purposes He knows long before we are born, even while we are formed in our mothers' wombs. HaShem knows us full well, as Melekh David used to say. Tzakhi's ima was a righteous woman, a daughter of the tribe of Benjamin, may her memory be for blessing."

More ameins.

Avidan said, "Before we go to wash and refresh ourselves, I will say this. Tzakhi's silver hair is a sign for all to read. He is old in wisdom. He fought trained fighters and prevailed with bow and sword. He fought also with his hands, and we bring you a captive as evidence he took no life unnecessarily. He trained animals to serve his battle plans. You yourselves know his donkey Baka brought the news of Nachshon's whereabouts. While Melekh Shlomo's armies were riding toward Ashur, Tzakhi alone knew the Arava and those who live here. HaShem aged Tzakhi ben Nachshon to fight with the venom of a serpent, the sting of the scorpion, the cunning of a wolf, and in the shadow of a tzirah. HaShem knew the exact moment He would call Tzakhi to battle for his father. Now, what does the Holy Scroll say of one with white hair?"

"We should rise in his presence to honor him," said The Levite.

Ameins.

"I'm not asking you to rise in Tzakhi's presence," said Captain Avidan, "because he is still a youth in years, but I'm asking you to honor his faithfulness to HaShem, his father, and to our Melekh Shlomo. I say *todah rabbah*[38] to him now publicly, for restoring my son to me."

The captain pressed his hand to heart and nodded in gratefulness to Tzakhi. Tzakhi returned the gesture, saying, *"B'vakasha. B'keif."*[39]

Abba had been quiet, his big, burn-scarred hand resting on Shira's shoulder, but now he spoke up. "Tonight, we tell the story with a feast!" He turned toward the steward over the fortress' livestock. "Tender lamb and goat to feed everyone. Let the women bring their best dishes and sweets to share. It will be a feast of thanksgiving for Tamar before we depart for the great feast in Yerushalayim." Abba found the ration steward standing in the crowd. "And our best wine and oil to make us glad in our salvation!"

"Amein!"

"Baruch HaShem!"

"Kol ha-kvod!"[40]

---

38 Thank you very much.
39 You're welcome. With pleasure.
40 Glory!

CHAPTER FORTY-NINE

Yerushalayim was even more glorious than Tzakhi had imagined. Many of the buildings were new. It was truly a city of gold. When the sun set, its pink stone buildings glowed like gold, just as glorious as the gold in Melekh Shlomo's palace and the Holy Temple.

They were to be honored guests of the melekh during the second day of Sukkot, and the royal chamberlain had ordered their assigned steward to supply him and Abba each with a fine purple linen garment, including new bright white linen turbans. All his brothers received such a robe from the melekh once per year. Tzakhi wound his turban around to conceal his hair. Abba wore his turban loosely over his head with only a leather band to hold it in place like the other men. It was nice to see Abba without his leather fire-helmet.

Abba said Yerushalayim was even more lively than usual due to the presence of the queen, Malkhat Sheva, in the city. She and her retinue required many attendants, and Melekh Shlomo was quite smitten with her. And she with him. What the Egyptian wife thought of that was the talk of the city.

Malkhat Sheva brought him many priceless gifts, among them a beautiful mare of Arabian stock named Safanad. The mare was so valuable that she had both personal grooms and bodyguards.

She was fed the finest of wheat, oats, and barley, and only the cleanest of tender grass hay passed her soft lips.

The queen's most priceless gifts were precious balsam plants, for which Melekh Shlomo had set aside a special place near Ein Gedi to cultivate. It was on the road from Tamar to Yerushalayim, so Tzakhi would be able to stop in during his feast pilgrimages to see the progress of the valuable spice plants.

Accustomed to early rising, Abba woke Tzakhi to go with him to morning prayers in the Temple while the morning *tamid* sacrifice was offered. They were all staying in a house Abba rented for the feasts. At dawn, Abba, Tzakhi, and his brothers joined the queue at the mikveh, a great pool of water for ritual immersion in the City of David. From there, they would ascend the steep steps to the Temple Mount together.

This was the first time Tzakhi had mikveh'd. He was very glad it was only men there, for one had to disrobe completely to dip in the waters of the mikveh. Thankfully, there were privacy screens. His silver hair was not all Tzakhi preferred to keep private.

Tzakhi was the last of his brothers to immerse, and after he re-dressed, Abba placed some coins in his hand. "This is compensation for the work you lost while you searched for me. You must not appear before HaShem empty-handed, so decide what you will give to the Holy Temple. There will be a place to put the money when we enter the outer courtyard. The containers look like trumpets turned on their ends."

"Yes, Abba."

"The Levite explained the sacrifices to you well?" Abba asked.

"Yes, Abba."

"In the future, if you want to present a sacrifice, there are other places to purchase them, but you will see pens of unblemished animals along the ascent to the Holy Mountain. The Levites also have inspected animals, and you can purchase one once we reach the top. It is much tidier than dragging them yourself, and less stressful for the animals," said Abba.

Abba had shown Tzakhi how to kosher-slaughter an animal when he was very young, and he understood. If the knife were properly sharp, and the cut skillful, the animal walked a few steps and kind of fainted, never really knowing what happened. The key was doing it while the animal was relaxed and remaining relaxed yourself. Watching the post-mortem muscle jerks was worse than the cut itself.

Tzakhi didn't like killing animals, but he did like to eat. He was glad he wasn't a shepherd. It would be difficult to slaughter an animal you'd cared for it all its life. If he hadn't feared for his own life and Abba's, Tzakhi didn't know how he'd have shot the man-stealers on Har Karkom.

"The crowds are so great today because it is the first day of the feast," said Abba, climbing the steps. "Tomorrow is our audience with Melekh Shlomo. On the third day of the feast, you will put on tefillin for the first time. We are invited to share the melekh's table tomorrow, but on the day we offer a sacrifice, we'll give portions to the priests and Levites first, and then roast it in the community oven near our rented house. We'll invite friends and even strangers to share it."

"Who will cook?" asked Tzakhi.

"There are women who prepare cooked food," said Abba.

"It is a *chag*, but the women work?" asked Tzakhi.

Abba looked annoyed. "Would you have a man do a woman's work?"

Tzakhi started to argue, but decided it wasn't the place or the time. There never was a place or time to argue with Abba.

One of his older brothers spoke up. "Men work, too, Tzakhi. They built our sukkah, and they manage all the animals for sacrifice and the animals people ride here. The people of Yerushalayim are very generous at the feasts. And the women don't cook on the Shabbat Shabbaton. They serve what is already prepared and held warm."

That made more sense. Weekly Shabbats were like that. And the Arava was a perfect place to keep foods warm most of the year.

Tzakhi was in good physical shape, but these steep steps to the Temple were a challenge. Some pilgrims were cautious, picking their way carefully and not wasting their breath on small talk, but others were much more confident, climbing and singing with the ease of mountain goats.

When their little band finally attained the Temple Mount plateau and entered the gate, Tzakhi inhaled deeply. Indeed, there was something here. A much stronger Presence than what he had felt at Har Karkom. It was like an unseen Hand pushed him down, but not in an unpleasant way. If the wilderness dead whispered from just on the other side of the veil at Tamar, then here there was something that was life itself. It was the beginning of breath.

The Temple Mount was above Yerushalayim, but there was something higher, some activity Tzakhi strained to see above them, but he only saw blue sky and scattered white, fluffy clouds. Smoke from the inner court rose in an odd way, not dissipating like normal smoke, but seeming to gather instead, rising up straight like a pillar, impervious to the wind that should blow it away. The smell of incense hung heavy as well.

It was in the crowded Great Courtyard that Abba showed Tzakhi where he'd receive his own tefillin, the small, rectangular leather pouches containing the words from the Torah. The *shel rosh* would be held in place by a headband, and the *shel yad* was held on the bicep by seven wraps of a strap down his arm, then looped around the fingers.

Once his tefillin were in place, Abba would bless him by pressing his big, scarred hands on Tzakhi's head. He would pronounce words of peace, prosperity, safety, and happiness. His brothers would dance around him and pronounce him a "Ben Torah," a son of the commandment. Being the son of the Torah and Nachshon was a lot to carry on your head or your arm. Tzakhi was glad Abba was walking him through the ceremony beforehand.

The Temple Mount was magnificent, thousands upon thousands of voices singing, shouting, waving fragrant lulavs,[41] murmuring through portions of the prayers, clapping, jumping, dancing. Yes, Tzakhi felt the Holy Presence much heavier here than Har Karkom, but it wasn't frightening. It was as if heavenly joy had become a cloud one could stand in on earth.

After the morning sacrifice was completed, Abba guided Tzakhi back to the Great Courtyard where all could mingle. There were groups of people sitting and talking. In some of the groups, a scribe, or *sofer*, held a scroll of the Torah while the group discussed it. Abba looked around, maybe for someone in particular, and then Ovadyah touched his shoulder and pointed to a scribe sitting in the shade of the wall with a small group. "There he is," said Ovadyah. "The Levite's brother."

Abba made his way to the little group, and Tzakhi and his brothers followed. "This sofer is excellent," Ovadyah assured Tzakhi. "He won't try to scare your breakfast out of you."

"It might be too late," joked Tzakhi. Ovadyah was the brother who would joke with him.

---

41   "The Four Species" of tree branches waved at the Feast of Sukkot

Abba found a place for them near the sofer, and they all sat and listened for several minutes.

It was the holy scroll of Shemot under discussion, a section called Mishpatim, or "Judgments." Oh, no. The legal parts of the Holy Torah were difficult. It took lots of clarification by The Levite. Every single word, every letter, mattered. The stories of Bereishit were much easier to understand. Tzakhi listened while the sofer questioned the group about the commandment not to give a false testimony.

Three other boys about Tzakhi's age sat at the front, and when the sofer paused to move on to a new law, he motioned Tzakhi forward solemnly. *He really does look like The Levite. Just as serious about the Torah, too.* When Tzakhi re-seated himself, he saw the other boys looked as scared as he felt. An extra year of preparation didn't give Tzakhi extra confidence.

The sofer stood, and everyone stood with him. He unrolled the scroll and read the next law:

> *You shall not go after the many to do evil,*
> *And you shall not answer over a dispute to tilt after the many.*[42]

"Amein," said the sofer.

"Amein," responded the group.

Uh oh. There was something about that law, a clarification that had stumped Tzakhi. His mind tended to wander to what might be going on in the horse pens or when the saffron-crocuses might bloom so he could beat the sharp-eyed Kenite boys in collecting the delicate saffron to sell. He couldn't afford to let his mind wander now. His brothers would never let him forget it.

---

42   Exodus 23:2 (Artscroll)

The sofer rolled up the scroll and sat again. The group sat, too. The sofer asked, "First, what is the context? What is the rule?"

"Witnessing in court," called out Elad. "Explanation obtained from context. *Davar hilmad me'anino.*"

The boys nodded their heads vigorously as if they already knew that. They should. That was an easy question. One of the boys added, "It speaks of capital cases before the court."

The sofer blinked, not too impressed with comprehension of the obvious. He then looked at Tzakhi more closely. The silver pe-ot. He'd thought to tuck them in like he normally did, but this was a religious feast, and wearing his pe-ot untrimmed was a commandment. It seemed proper to leave them neatly curled, but loose. Unfazed by a boy with the hair of an old man, the sofer asked Tzakhi the next question directly. "What does it mean, 'you shall not respond over a dispute'? This is strange wording, yes?"

Ugh. That was the hard part. Thank Heaven The Levite was a hard teacher. "The difficult words are *ta-aneh al rav*," said Tzakhi. "'Answer against the many.' It can also mean, 'answer against the great one.' It means a lesser judge cannot argue against a greater judge."

"Why not?" asked the sofer. He looked around, but no one else volunteered the answer.

Tzakhi took a deep breath and said, "A judge is worthy of respect. A more honorable judge must not be disrespected by a lesser judge responding to his answer to acquit or convict in front of him. But fairness is the most important thing in a capital case. It is judged by twenty-three judges. The case may be tilted to convict by a majority of two judges, but it may be tilted to acquit by a majority of only one judge. If a judge errs, then grace is extended in favor of acquittal to prevent the death sentence being imposed on an innocent man. That's why it takes more judges to convict than to acquit."

There was a low murmur of approval in the group, which had grown simply because Nachshon and his brawny, red-haired, purple-clad sons sat there.

"Well-stated," said the sofer. "But finish your first thought. What does a judge's status have to do with tilting the verdict in a capital case?"

All three of the other boys looked at Tzakhi, a little relieved and a little gloating that the show-off was about to be cut down to size.

Tzakhi took a breath, searching his memory. It helped if he added the persistent, tumultuous chatter of sparrows in the tamarisk trees near the well at Tamar along with the breeze stirring the odor of donkeys and camels. He answered, "The greater judge's status might influence a lesser, more inexperienced judge. A younger judge might be awed by the wisdom of a great scholar. This could sway his opinion. He might be too embarrassed to argue his opinion honestly before a great one, or he might be humiliated by others for contradicting a great one."

Another boy piped up, "Or if he is impudent, he might argue against the greater judge to whiten his face!"

Silence followed, and the boy glanced left and right without moving his head to read the reaction of the group.

The sofer said, "Excellent thoughts. Continue. How is this problem resolved by our text?"

The other boy was silent, but Tzakhi had pulled up the well-bucket of memory completely now, and he repeated the words of The Levite: "In such a case, they poll the judges beginning with the lesser ones. The younger judges will give their explanation and verdict, then leave. The oldest, most respected judge will be polled last. This way, the younger are not swayed to tilt the judgment in the direction of the great ones, and they are encouraged to give their arguments for conviction or acquittal freely. Younger members never dispute an opinion already stated by an older member of the court. It maintains the integrity of the court's verdicts as well as the honor of its members. In capital cases, a person's life hangs in the balance. This is the best way to do justice instead of evil."

The sofer's serious face broke into a toothy smile, and the group cheered: "*Ben ha-Torah! Ben ha-Torah!*"

From behind, one of his brothers pushed him playfully. Tzakhi couldn't rejoice yet. One more question could sink him.

Oh please, let this be over. I can't take much more of this.

"I can see you are ready to explore Yerushalayim," the sofer said to Tzakhi, including the other boys in his approving gaze. "Please go rejoice before HaShem and give a few more lads an opportunity to make me marvel at their wisdom."

Tzakhi and the other three boys nearly knocked heads trying to scramble up, which made the group laugh.

The sofer looked over the crowd at Abba. "You bring me news of my brother Kohat?"

So The Levite had a name! Kohat.

"Ken, Eli," said Abba, who stood. "I brought you a parcel of parchments and spices. Even a special ink Kohat purchased from far eastern traders. And I hope you have letters I can return to him. He is always hungry for news. You are welcome to our sukkah this week. We have an audience with Melekh Shlomo tomorrow, but the following morning, I'm purchasing Temple tokens for a bull to sacrifice and for libations. We'll have much food to share. Captain Avidan and I have set aside money to commission you with a new scroll of Bereishit for Tamar. We could discuss this with you, perhaps persuade you to deliver it yourself."

"Yes, I heard," said Eli. "And this must be the young silver-haired desert wolf who conquered Amalek, Edom, and Egypt."

"The very one, Eli," Abba said, smiling.

"*L'hitraot*,[43] Nachshon," said the scribe.

"*L'hitraot*, Eli."

---

43 See you later.

CHAPTER FIFTY

After the morning sacrifice, prayers, and discussion of the Holy Scroll, together they walked the streets. Abba's four bodyguards re-joined them at the bottom of the magnificent steps leading up to the Temple. Although armed with spears and short swords, they looked fresher than usual. Their scale armor, shields, and helmets were cleaned of dust, polished, and well-oiled, and they wore new sandals with the long shin guards. Tzakhi didn't know how they could concentrate on protecting Abba with so much going on around them.

Spontaneously, men would make a circle and dance while they sang, waving and shaking lulavs and passing them to onlookers. Crowds encouraged men doing acrobatics. Some juggled eggs or pottery. Children ran everywhere.

A donkey trotted through the crowd, riderless. Dogs ran and barked, and the sparrows were numerous, their cheerful chittering competing with the street noise. Cats watched from the safety of windows and rooftops or darted through the legs of the pilgrims in the streets.

Although Elad was the oldest and walked on Abba's right, and Ovadyah was the next oldest, it was Tzakhi whom Abba kept close at his left hand so he could explain everything. When the donkey trotted by, Abba said, "I missed you after you trained Baka to travel up the givah by herself. It was something I looked forward to each day."

Tzakhi didn't know that.

"I think I fed her too many dates and scratched her ears too much when you didn't come up. Maybe that's why she returned to Tamar so fast from Karkom," he added with something like humor.

"Did you hear? Abba jested with Tzakhi!" Ovadyah announced to his brothers. "Are we not jealous now? We must certainly sell him to Ishmaelite traders going to Egypt."

This made them all laugh, and Abba held up his hand, circling his thumb with his forefingers in feigned exasperation.

Many people were giving away food or sweets, sharing their holy offerings. They searched especially for those who weren't dressed as well or the disabled, who were sitting on mats near the gates. Some of the needy were already surrounded by piles of fig cakes, raisin cakes, breads, juglets of date honey, and even dried or pickled fish.

A small band of Hittite men marched north through the street, each carrying bundles or leading donkeys laden with burdens. They were supervised by men carrying rods. "Why are Hittites carrying burdens like servants on a Shabbat Shabbaton?"[44] asked Tzakhi.

"They *are* servants," said Elad. "Melekh Shlomo forced labor upon the Hittites, Perizzites, Hivites, and other Canaanites. He dismissed the Israelite forced laborers after they completed The House of the Forest of Lebanon, his smaller palaces, and the Holy Temple, but he kept the Canaanites working."

---

44   High sabbath, special feast day

"I heard the northern tribes are not happy even though they are now released from supplying workers," said Tzakhi.

"I imagine you hear a lot of things at the caravansary and from the soldiers," said Abba, maybe smiling a little. "Twenty years is a long levy for unpaid labor. They feel like Judah and Benjamin are benefiting the most, maybe the building was simply to satisfy Melekh Shlomo's vanity. And many do not want to travel all the way to Yerushalayim for the three feasts. It was easier for them to travel to Shiloh before the Temple was built. Many were sacrificing on the high places so they wouldn't have to travel at all."

Ovadyah added, "And the Hittites are uneasy as well. Some of them carry a grudge against Melekh David for causing Bat-Sheva's[45] husband to be killed in battle. He was a Hittite and served Melekh David perfectly and faithfully. Bat-Sheva's son forcing them to labor in Melekh David's city is a continued insult."

"What do you think, Abba? Was it wrong to force the men to work? And on a *chag*?" asked Tzakhi. "Even servants are supposed to stop their labors."

"It's not for me to second-guess the king's decisions, Tzakhi. The amount of bronze needed for the Temple was so great that it's consumed all my uncles, brothers, nephews, and sons for twenty years. We had work, but the work was hard. I wish I had spent more time with you all. A few weeks swimming in the summer and the feast pilgrimages were not much time. I feel like I hardly know my sons apart from the work."

Tzakhi had never heard Abba say such a thing. Was it the long days thinking he was about to be separated from his sons forever?

Or was it the milling families in Yerushalayim who were laughing, eating, carrying children on their shoulders? The delight

---

45　Bathsheba

in the faces of those seeing others whom they saw only a few times per year? Maybe the lofty, distant voices of the Levitical choir on the Temple Mount?

Tzakhi's brothers cast looks at one another, as if they had the same thoughts, but dared not say them aloud. It gave Tzakhi courage. "Abba, I don't want to apprentice to the fires," said Tzakhi. He said it simply. Not boldly, but not hesitantly. "I am afraid of them. I don't know why. But I know I'm not like my brothers. It's not just my hair."

Abba stopped and looked down at him. Abba was a head taller than most men, and he was strong, even in his fifty-fourth year. Although his extra year had given him time to grow taller, and his muscles were firm from lifting baggage, Tzakhi was still more than a handbreadth shorter than Abba. Tzakhi looked up, meeting Abba's eyes, something few people could...or would.

His brothers surrounded them protectively from the crowd's surges, forming a barrier. The sons of Nachshon. Tall, powerful, fiery-haired, and formidable like their abba. And then there was Tzakhi. Slim, hair of a sage, a killer of man-stealers, a desert wolf.

The hard lines of Abba's bronze facial skin didn't contract like they did when he was displeased. Instead, he looked relieved. "I'm glad, Tzakhi. I delayed your apprenticeship to give us both some extra time to think about your trade."

Tzakhi could have fallen over from relief. Instead, he took a bite out of a bit of gifted grilled lamb on a stick and nodded to smooth out the knot in his throat. His brothers exchanged more knowing glances. Not unkind ones, though.

"You're afraid of the fires because you nearly burned when you were just an infant. See these scars?" asked Abba. He flipped both arms so his palms pointed downward.

Tzakhi nodded again. They were the worst scars. Deep ones, not the random firebrands.

"You were asleep in your bed when an oil lamp broke in its wall niche and caught the insect drape around your bed on fire. I pulled it away and dragged it out of the house, and it fell across my arms. After that, the fires did not seem like a place you should be."

"But Abba, when I asked you before, you acted as though you wouldn't let me scout or be a soldier," said Tzakhi.

"That's because Melekh Shlomo has demanded so much of us. I had already saved Salmah from the furnace, but I didn't think the melekh would let another son leave the trade. His demand for bronze and iron is..."

Abba looked around, then fell silent as if someone might be listening. A small motion with his chin stopped the line of conversation. "He sent me Shira. Maybe he thinks I will live long enough to father and train more sons. It would be nice to have a daughter, though. I've always wanted one."

Ovadyah patted Tzakhi's cheeks. "Tzakhi's growing a beard already. You'd better hurry, Abba. He won't be pretty much longer."

Tzakhi had been the youngest all his life. It would be strange to have a younger brother or sister. Not bad, just strange. A sister like Shira would be nice.

CHAPTER FIFTY-ONE

Although he wore a clean turban and purple, those who passed by looked at Nachshon's short beard curiously, then looked away when they saw the accompanying sons and bodyguards. Forge workers couldn't grow long hair. Royal silversmiths and goldsmiths all stood out in a crowd, but only the keeper of the copper and iron fires needed protection.

The heavy thought of the Kittim, Yavan, Ashur, or other armies preparing to invade Israel finally sank down upon Tzakhi's heart. He'd pushed it away while he searched for Abba. The reason for the kidnapping was not as important as finding Abba. He'd even pushed away thoughts of the desert hunt while he prepared for the journey to Yerushalayim with Abba. Once surrounded by his brothers on the trip, it was easy to keep pushing away the thoughts. Now the crowds pulled it all together for him.

He'd known all his thinking life that Abba's work was extremely valuable, but now he could see it. Israel was full of people, not like the sparsely populated Arava. If ships full of Kitti soldiers landed on the coast, and those soldiers had stronger spears and swords, Israel could be lost. It would be the same if Ashur's king and nobles fought less with one another and assembled their growing army to seek the secrets of hardened iron swords.

So many people. Not just the melekh's workers and soldiers like Tamar. Not the Midianites and Bedouin in their tents who would melt away in the safety of the desert at the first sign of trouble. There were more women and children here in Yerushalayim than Tzakhi had ever imagined.

All of Melekh Shlomo's treaties and alliances would collapse in a moment if other kingdoms saw an opportunity to benefit from Israel's trouble. The trade routes they coveted were too great a prize. Greed was so much more powerful than loyalty to covenants. Peace was a precariously balanced product. Even Pharaoh was gambling some shekels in the game. Harboring Sar Hadad and encouraging him to rival Melekh Shlomo in trade was neither ignorance nor an idle gambit.

Melekh Shlomo's reign was like having a weight balance with multiple pans. It wasn't like the moneychangers' balances with two pans, and all that needed to be done was to remove weight or add to one pan until they balanced. The king was trying to balance dozens of them. Tzakhi almost felt sorry for him, but Shira's face floated before him. *Whatever else would I want, Tzakhi?*

The price of this kingdom was ultimately not the silver, gold, bronze weapons, spices, dyes, or cloth. It traded in human souls. The hundreds of women housed in the king's palaces were trade goods. They helped Melekh Shlomo and the kingdoms from which they were gifted to balance all their pans of commerce and security. Tzakhi was no expert in the Holy Torah, but he knew this was wrong.

The Levite taught Tzakhi that peace is something that must be made. It does not dwell naturally among human beings or animals. It had to be built like a wall or crafted like a piece of jewelry. Peace never made itself. Even if it seemed there was peace, war was only hiding, waiting for a chance to take the naïve by surprise. But even The Levite had offered no homily, no comment to the passage when Tzakhi had read it aloud from the little scroll of Devarim:

When you enter the land which the LORD your God gives you, and you possess it and live in it, and you say, 'I will set a king over me like all the nations who are around me,' you shall surely set a king over you whom the LORD your God chooses, one from among your countrymen you shall set as king over yourselves; you may not put a foreigner over yourselves who is not your countryman. Moreover, he shall not multiply horses for himself, nor shall he cause the people to return to Egypt to multiply horses, since the LORD has said to you, 'You shall never again return that way.' He shall not multiply wives for himself, or else his heart will turn away; nor shall he greatly increase silver and gold for himself.

Now it shall come about when he sits on the throne of his kingdom, he shall write for himself a copy of this law on a scroll in the presence of the Levitical priests. It shall be with him and he shall read it all the days of his life, that he may learn to fear the LORD his God, by carefully observing all the words of this law and these statutes, that his heart may not be lifted up above his countrymen and that he may not turn aside from the commandment, to the right or the left, so that he and his sons may continue long in his kingdom in the midst of Israel.[46]

The countrymen forced to labor on the king's building projects were not volunteers, but a living tax levied upon the tribes of Israel.

---

46 Deuteronomy 17:14-20

Such a thought was probably treasonous. And it was much too complicated for Tzakhi to organize his thoughts about it. Now that he might not have to go to the fires, maybe he could go to the coast to learn administration with Barzillai, his lame brother. It was a place of many peoples assembled from afar, like Tamar. Now he only had one thought. Where was Salmah?

At first, Abba seemed not to notice Salmah's absence, but as they spent the day visiting friends and extended family, walking the streets of Yerushalayim, Tzakhi thought maybe Abba looked around more than usual. He was tall enough to see over most in a crowd. But Abba never did see Salmah.

CHAPTER FIFTY-TWO

Toward evening, Abba clapped Tzakhi on the shoulder. "Why so serious? It's time to feast."

Tzakhi tried to smile. "Where is Salmah?"

Elad spoke up, "He's probably up on the Temple Mount with the prophets. He may have been there this morning while we were there. There are so many groups and gates that it's easy to miss someone."

"He knows his way to the house we rent for the feasts. I'm sure he'll be there," said Abba.

"But you and I will be at the palace tomorrow," said Tzakhi. "What if we miss him?"

"Sukkot lasts for eight days," said Barzillai, who was sweating from the effort of walking the cobbled streets with his crutch all day while they visited with men Tzakhi had never met. "He'll wander in eventually. Salmah is Salmah."

In the approaching twilight, sellers had begun to replace those giving away food. Abba touched Elad's shoulder and nodded toward a street vendor setting up baked goods in a sukkah. "Please, ask for a full platter so there is enough *kunafe* for everyone who might join us tonight after the meat has passed from our stomachs. That baker has the finest in all Yerushalayim, better even than those sold in the *shuk*. He knows me. Tell him we will return his platter and jug with payment tomorrow morning."

Ovadyah went with Elad. Elad returned with a huge platter of pastries, and Ovadyah carried a small jug of honey and rosewater to be heated and drizzled over the pastries once they warmed for a short time in the oven. It was Tzakhi's favorite sweet.

The full moon made it easy to find their way. "They'll light torches along the streets soon," Uri told Tzakhi. "The moon...the torches...the singing echoing in the streets...the smell of roasted meat...you'll look forward to this every time you come for the chagim."

They entered the courtyard of the cluster of homes, one of which their family used at the three pilgrimage festivals of Pesach, Shavuot, and Sukkot. Decorated sukkot filled the courtyard and sat atop the roofs.

Each sukkah was supported by sturdier limbs or boards, but the crossbeams of the roofs were cut from mere saplings, and they were thinly covered in palm branches. Someone had hung various dried fruits from the palm branches. Straw mats and soft cushions lined the insides for sitting, eating, and sleeping.

Abba went to talk to the man who tended the covered pit where the lambs and goats had been roasting since the day before, even great shanks of beef. The community oven's small opening still emitted heat along with wonderful cooking smells, and clay pots lined along its ledges, keeping warm.

Barzillai went to their sukkah, collapsing on a cushion. Another brother drew some cool water out of a big jug sitting in the shade and took it to him. Pinchas and Natan helped a man lighting torches and lamps in the courtyard.

Elad and Ovadyah set the pastries and honey on a ledge around the oven for later. A woman emerged from their rental home, noticed the Nachshon family had arrived, and went back inside briefly. When she returned, she threw a light cheesecloth over the honey, but not the pastries. "The bees don't eat much," explained Ovadyah, "but we can't let bugs die in the honey. They come to the torches."

Tzakhi nodded. No Israelite could drink or eat from a vessel where something had crawled in and died. He definitely didn't want to risk ruining the honey topping on his favorite sweet. He'd sniffed the honey jug, and there was a slight scent of rosewater. Shira loved rosewater, sometimes adding it to her freshly-laundered clothes or to her and Abba's sleeping blanket. Tzakhi wasn't sure why Abba tolerated it. It wasn't very manly.

After everyone had washed their feet in a low basin set aside for that, they also washed their hands in a large, low-rimmed bowl. While they washed, the man minding the roasting pit removed two large lamb shoulders and began carving them on a wooden table set up nearby. There was no real cutting to do. The meat fell apart because it had slow-roasted for a full day. He placed the chunks on large platters on the ledge near the oven to keep them warm.

One by one, the brothers made their way to the sukkah, and the woman brought them cups of cool, spiced pomegranate wine. For once, Tzakhi wasn't served the watered-down version. It was a commandment of the Holy Torah to drink wine or strong drink at Sukkot. This was strong.

A girl about Tzakhi's age helped the woman. Maybe her daughter?

"Who's she?" Tzakhi asked Uri, the brother next to him. It should have been Salmah, the next to youngest. The brothers all sat in birth order according to the tradition.

Uri smiled. "She's pretty, yes?"

Tzakhi nodded. Uri said, "A few whiskers on your cheeks and a swallow of wine, and already you're looking for a match?"

"But who is she?" persisted Tzakhi.

Instead of answering, Uri turned and whispered loudly to the brother next to him that Tzakhi thought the girl was pretty. From there, it went around the table all the way to Elad, who declined to pass it on to Abba. Family meals with his brothers usually went like this, but it was the first time he'd been teased about a girl.

After everyone finished their first cup of wine, Abba signaled they should sit around the low table. The serving woman...her name was Sarah...and the girl had set the table with many dishes: olives, pickled cucumber with dill, almonds and pistachios, pomegranates, figs, fine wheat breads, little bowls of aged grape vinegar, smoked fish, tachina dips, cold pumpkin cubes with a vinegary-sweet spice sauce, simmered molokhia greens, sweet melon, savory lentils and beans, and fritters with spiced ground meat and wheat inside.

Tzakhi was honored to say the kiddush, the wine blessing, since it was his special day. He lifted his cup of grape wine and said the special festival blessing ending with, "Blessed are you, O Lord our God, King of the Universe, Who creates the fruit of the vine."

"Amein," responded everyone who heard it, even those milling in the courtyard who weren't in the sukkah.

The serving woman brought another basin of water around, and everyone briefly washed his hands ceremonially, not to clean them, but similar to how the priests washed in the Temple before they started their service.

Afterward, Abba salted and held up two loaves of fine wheat bread. He said another blessing, "Blessed are you, O Lord our God, King of the Universe, Who brings forth the bread from the earth."

"Amein," everyone responded again in the torch-light.

Abba broke the bread, ate a morsel, then handed it to Elad, who passed it down until everyone had torn off a piece and eaten. The pitmaster brought the platters of mustard-and-garlic roasted lamb and set them on the low table, which could hold not one more dish afterward.

They all tore into the food, hungry from the long day.

Suddenly, Tzakhi heard something familiar over the many conversations around the table, in the courtyard, and the din from the street.

A flute.

He froze, listening. He'd heard many flutes, but this was a tune only Tzakhi would recognize. Only he knew the words. *So long ago, so long ago...*

Tzakhi leaped up and ran to the courtyard door. Salmah moved the flute away from his lips and smiled, opening his arms wide.

CHAPTER FIFTY-THREE

Salmah was very mysterious, more than usual. All he'd say was some small rebellion was fomenting against Melekh Shlomo in Beit El. Because the school of the prophets was there, they were suspected of involvement and were frequently spied upon by the melekh's agents. Salmah therefore decided not to join the family until after their meeting at the Holy Temple so he wouldn't be followed on holy ground. Tzakhi and Salmah talked rapidly, catching up on their years apart.

"*Nachshon, charash roshi shel Melekh Shlomo!*" a deep bass voice called out at the gate into the courtyard.

Abba, Tzakhi, and his brothers all looked up from the rich goat cheese pastries, their chins and beards shining with drops of fragrant honey. It was fully dark, but the torches in the walls lit the courtyard. There was less milling about now, but laughter and songs still rang through the streets as families and groups talked and sang in their sukkot. Tzakhi wiped honey from his fingers with a wet cloth and loosened his knife in its scabbard.

Two of Abba's bodyguards sat in the sukkah on cushions eating, but the two who stood watch instantly lowered their spears in the direction of the strong voice.

Whoever it was calling for Nachshon must have seen the guards in the torch-light. "May I enter?" the voice boomed. "It is I, Naftali ben Sapir. The master teller of stories."

One of the guards looked at Abba.

"Let him enter," said Abba. "I knew this would come. These storytellers walk the streets of Yerushalayim at the feasts seeking stories to tell in the town squares and on the highways. It's like the caravans, people will throw a coin for a good story, true or not."

Abba locked his eyes onto Tzakhi's. "I want this story to be told as far as Kittim," he said. "Don't leave out anything."

Tzakhi understood. This story could make the Kittim hesitant to tangle with him again if they thought he had supernatural powers.

The storyteller Naftali ben Sapir found his way to their sukkah, a guard on either side of him. "So is it true?" Naftali asked Abba. "You were stolen by Amalekites?"

Naftali was dressed in a rough, hooded tunic, but it was not worn or unclean, at least as much as Tzakhi could tell in the full moonlight and torchlight.

"Ken," said Abba. "Please, sit. Have you eaten a meal? Would you like some sweets and wine?"

Normally, it was probably the last thing Abba wanted to offer to the storyteller, but this story might be a wall of safety around Tzakhi and Salmah as formidable as the walls of Yerushalayim itself. And it was a *mitzvah*[47] to offer hospitality at Sukkot.

Tzakhi had just finished his second cup of grape wine, and he was feeling merry and very hospitable.

---

47   Commandment, good deed

"Only diluted wine for me," said Naftali. "What I really want is to hear the story if you will tell me. It is already being told, but I'm sure you'd rather it be told factually instead of fancifully."

"What story is this?" Salmah asked Tzakhi. "Stolen by what Amalekites?"

"You really have been in the cave of the prophets," muttered Tzakhi.

Abba adjusted himself on a cushion. "I can tell you a little," he said. "But Tzakhi will have to tell most of it. You might be here until midnight."

The serving woman brought a cup of wine, poured a little water in it, and handed it to Naftali. Tzakhi was disappointed the pretty girl was no longer serving. She must have retired for the night to their roof. Ovadyah said they stayed there during Sukkot in order to rent out their house like lots of other families in Yerushalayim. Or sometimes families rented out the roof or upper rooms instead.

Uri, who was reclining, pushed out a spare cushion to the storyteller with his foot. "I've been waiting to hear the whole story myself," he said. Uri worked in the eastern plains of the Yarden River preparing copper vessels for the melekh, so he'd not traveled with them from the Arava. He'd missed the story.

The storyteller had an interesting way of memorizing the tale. When Abba would pause, which most people did as they spoke to collect their next thoughts, Naftali would repeat what he'd just said, word-for-word. The difference was he'd sing it. It made sense. It was a lot easier to remember songs than only words. The Levite taught Tzakhi to read the Holy Torah by chanting it. And as with the chants of the Holy Torah, the storyteller used many of the same notes over and over, rhythmically.

When it was Tzakhi's turn to take over the tale, he told it in little chunks, which helped Naftali echo his words. Salmah picked up his flute and played the notes. His finely-tuned ear had heard the storyteller's repetitions all the way down to the minor keys of danger notes. With the flute accompanying him, Naftali's repetitions alternating with Tzakhi's words created a mesmerizing song.

Everyone in the courtyard had gathered around their sukkah, even leaving their own sukkot to hear the tale. Someone started tapping the drumhead of a timbrel to the inflections of word and song.

The wine loosened Tzakhi's tongue, and the tale rolled out of him easily, even dramatically at times. Homing donkeys, tearing wolves, flying serpents, poison porcupines, and sand monsters paraded through the sukkah. So did a long-haired, throat-cutting Kitti, renegade Edomites, and drooling Amalekites. Then a fleet Egyptian mare pawed the sky and fled from a man who vaporized in Heavenly lightning and ice.

When the storyteller's gaze settled upon his silver pe-ot, the only hair showing beneath his turban, Tzakhi did not offer to show him the rest of his hair. He was no longer ashamed of it, but maybe the story would be better if people only wondered about it. There was a little shorn spot on the top of his head that had not yet grown in. That was the part of the story Tzakhi wished had not disappeared to the coastland of the Kittim. He must tell this story well.

Although the sukkah was lit only by moon and torchlight, Tzakhi saw Salmah's eyes fix on him when he came to the part where the Edomite pulled off his turban. The eyes glittered with sudden comprehension. *So long ago...*

CHAPTER FIFTY-FOUR

The stones of Melekh Shlomo's palace were as enormous as many of the Temple stones. The great hall called The Forest of Lebanon filled the whole palace with the clean, fresh scent of cedar. Great polished cedar ceiling beams rested on cedar pillars. Abba and Tzakhi waited there while the melekh finished his morning prayers in the Temple. There were special stairs leading directly from the palace to the Temple.

The Forest was paneled with cedar from floor to ceiling, which made the room feel cool, mysterious, and refined. Even the finest homes in the Arava had only lime plaster over the stone, not scented paneling.

The Lion-Throne in the Hall of Justice was more impressive even than the stories Tzakhi had heard of it. It was fashioned of ivory, much of it covered with gold. Set with rubies, sapphires, emeralds, and other precious stones, each shone with uniquely fascinating hues and colors.

Six steps led to the seat. According to the steward assigned to Tzakhi and Abba for the day, each step served to remind the melekh of one of the six special commandments that kings of Israel were to observe. The less Tzakhi thought about that, the better. Melekh Shlomo had re-interpreted them all.

On one edge of the first step, a golden lion lay facing a golden ox on the opposite side. On the second step, a golden wolf faced a golden lamb. On the third step, a golden tiger faced a golden camel. On the fourth, a golden eagle faced a golden peacock. On the fifth step, a golden cat faced a golden rooster. On the sixth, a golden hawk faced a golden dove. Above the throne, a golden dove held a golden hawk in its beak. The animals were so life-like, Tzakhi half-expected the golden wolf to turn her head and loll her tongue out at him.

Nearby stood a menorah of pure gold decorated with golden cups, knobs, flowers, blossoms, and petals. On each side of the throne there was a special golden chair, one for the High Priest, called the Kohen HaGadol, and one for the Segan, the assistant High Priest. There were also seventy golden chairs for the seventy judges of the Supreme Court. Today, there was no court sitting. Twenty-four golden vines branched into a huge canopy above the throne.

A flurry of activity and a trumpet signaled the arrival of the melekh from the Holy Temple. All bowed low and remained low as he entered with his attendants. Tzakhi, however, peeked up to watch. He'd heard fantastic things about the throne that didn't seem true. The only way to find out was to watch what happened.

When Melekh Shlomo stepped upon the first step up to the throne, the golden ox and the golden lion each stretched out one foot to support him and help him rise to the next step. What kind of mechanism was this? Egyptian sand leverage? Tzakhi longed to see the interior workings, but he dared move nothing but his eyes.

Each step was the same. On each side, the animals helped the melekh up until he was comfortably seated upon the throne. Once the melekh was seated, a golden eagle lowered the great crown just above Melekh Shlomo's brow. The melekh was impeccably groomed and dressed with royal robes and sash. Not a thing was out of place. At a signal, everyone was allowed to straighten.

No one was allowed in the melekh's presence unless he was clad in a clean linen garment. Abba and Tzakhi wore their gifted purple robes over their tunics. Melekh Shlomo himself was wearing the royal bluish-purple robe over a tunic of blue and his many-jeweled crown. It must have been an enormous weight. Maybe that's why the eagle held it just above his head. His hair and beard showed a little gray, yet both were trimmed and shiny, probably with fragrant oil.

A row of scribes sat to the melekh's left, each with his own kit of parchments, ink, scraping tool, and feathers. The melekh was quite the writer and composer, and Tzakhi had heard that when the melekh had some important or great thought, scribes were ever-present to record his wisdom or the lines of a poem or song.

The Chief Steward announced with a voice that boomed and echoed through the large palace: "Nachshon, Master Metalworker of Eretz Yisrael and Melekh Shlomo, and Tzakhi ben Nachshon."

"What gift may I bestow upon you, Tzakhi ben Nachshon?" asked Melekh Shlomo. A breathlessness fell over the grand throne room. Scribes leaned forward and held their quills at the ready.

That caught Tzakhi off guard. No one warned him the melekh would say such a thing. He dared not look at Abba for help. If he requested a position in the melekh's cavalry, was it a betrayal of his family?

"Melekhi..." said Tzakhi. The word came out thinly through the phlegm of uncertainty.

Melekh Shlomo smiled indulgently. He was probably used to this reaction.

"Your daughter, my abba's wife who lives with us at Tamar..."

The melekh's smile faded a little. He looked toward one of the scribes. "Her name is...?"

"Shira," answered the scribe.

"Yes, Shira," said Melekh Shlomo as if the scribe were the one who'd forgotten the name.

"Does she need a handmaiden? Servants? A physician?" asked the melekh.

"No, Melekhi," said Tzakhi. "She makes the most exquisite ointments and unguents from all the herbs and spices passing through on the caravans. I sell them, and together we do well. Some of the merchants like the small jars of ready-made products. They carry large quantities, but if they need to purchase or barter items along the way, the juglets are as good as coin. Sometimes they're better in places where there are no local compounders. Even here in Yerushalayim, the compounders sometimes have difficulty obtaining all the ingredients they need. At Tamar, everything passes through."

"What is it you're asking?" asked the melekh. "You want to peddle unguents in Yerushalayim?"

Beside him, Abba shifted a little. Tzakhi had better get to it.

"Melekhi, is it true there is a woman here in Yerushalayim who is one of your administrators? A high steward?" asked Tzakhi.

"Yes," said Melekh Shlomo. "Elichanah has her own signet. A very able administrator."

"Could you consider making Shira your administrator at Tamar? With a few of the melekh's servants, she could purchase from the supplies of spices before they reach Egypt, Ashdod, Tyre, or Yerushalayim. She could teach workers and oversee the compounding there. Beautiful Kenite pottery is always for sale at Tamar, and she could bargain for the jars and juglets. Whenever the tax detail travels to Yerushalayim, she could send finished products to the melekh's treasurer. They could return with some of the new pottery from the north of Israel we've seen. Those juglets, too, are very fine. It would enrich your majesty and give Israelites access to healing ointments at a cheaper price," said Tzakhi.

"Is my daughter not bearing you sons?" Melekh Shlomo asked Abba.

"Not yet, Melekhi. I am growing older," said Abba. "And I am absent much to supervise the smelting."

Melekh Shlomo leaned back on his throne, considering. Tzakhi appreciated Abba's answer. He'd not allowed Shira to take the blame for her childlessness. Most men assumed a woman who did not bear children, especially male children, had some defect or curse from Heaven.

"What would you think of such an arrangement?" the melekh asked Abba.

Abba hesitated only a moment before he said, "The two of them have filled a room of my house with their trade. I can't walk through the jars and pots and bundles. My home smells like the Yerushalayim *shuk*. They may as well do their marketing and conspiring in their own building."

The melekh suddenly sat up straight, eyes bright with an idea. "This is HaShem's parnasa, Nachshon."

Abba raised an eyebrow.

"Malkha Sheba has gifted us many balsam plants. We're starting an orchard of them near Ein Gedi. That's not far from you. You've heard of this, yes?"

Both Abba and Tzakhi nodded.

"I have much gold, but balsam is more valuable than gold. When the plants mature, I'll need someone trustworthy to oversee the compounding. I will not sell the product in bulk except to the Levites. I'm sending my own gardener to tend them because

I want to control the product from seed to final sale. It sounds as though Shira can ensure the security of the secrets of the various compounds. My own daughter would be loyal," said Melekh Shlomo.

A daughter whose name you didn't remember, thought Tzakhi.

The melekh thought for long seconds, perhaps scheming, planning, assigning work and resources. Finally, he looked at Abba. "You would approve of such a plan? You do not worry she would no longer want to warm your bed?"

"It is not a worry for me, Melekhi," said Abba. "I am quite warm already. Shira is not an arrogant girl. I am sure Shira can perform all her duties if she is given the resources and workers. If she is found with child, I'll hire a wet nurse. I already have grandsons who will be ready to apprentice soon. They can learn from her."

"If that is the situation," said Melekh Shlomo, "and your sons are competent...?"

"Yes, Melekhi," said Abba. "Especially Elad and Ovadyah. They manage smelting quality and procurement quite competently."

"Then you will reduce your travel for supervision to twice per year with a full detachment of soldiers. Remain at Tamar and continue experimenting with the iron smelting there on Givat Chatzeva. Bring Elad to Tamar and apprentice him to iron. Let him become your shadow, like Betzalel of blessed memory who remained in the shadow of El. And neither of you will stir from Tamar without a full detachment of horse soldiers and bodyguards. My steward will secure the extra horses and fodder."

"According to your will, Melekhi," Abba answered. A low murmur of affirmation from the court echoed through the great chamber.

Melekh Shlomo smiled and nodded to one of the scribes who was not yet writing. The scribe adjusted the writing desk in his lap and dipped his quill.

The melekh said, "So let it be written for the court. Prepare duplicate documents and deliver them to the steward over trade. I command he dispatch builders to Tamar after Sukkot to construct a spice house. He will construct based upon the design Shira requests. When it is complete, he will present a voucher to the Tamar tax administrator for enough coin to purchase the initial raw product, supplies, and the workers. Nachshon will bring Shira to the next feast, and I will discuss with her our plans for Ein Gedi when the balsam plants mature. Commission her a signet ring of onyx set in gold and a royal seal: 'Shira bat Melekh Shlomo.' In the meantime, I will dispatch an assistant to Shira because Tzakhi will not be able to continue doing her purchasing and bargaining."

Melekh Shlomo stopped and gazed at him.

Tzakhi wondered, *the fires*? After Abba had agreed he wasn't fit, was the melekh now about to assign him to one? Maybe he would apprentice to take the places of Elad or Ovadyah. He would spend his time pumping air into a furnace and turning rocks into ingots of pure copper. He hoped he could apprentice with Ovadyah, who oversaw the refining furnaces at Eilat and Etzion-Geber. At least Tzakhi could swim when he wasn't working.

CHAPTER FIFTY-FIVE

The melekh motioned to a different scribe, who removed a parchment from a small pile beside him. It already had writing on it.

Melekh Shlomo's handsome face suddenly looked despondent, dimming from the sheen of a new idea. He sagged a bit upon the great Lion-Throne. He said, "You, Tzakhi, will have to suffer for my mistakes. The wealth I've built will evaporate like morning dew upon a blade of grass. The price of building that wealth is already dividing my kingdom. Promise me, Tzakhi, you will serve my heir and preserve Judah and Benjamin. You understand the danger across The Great Sea and The Perat River. It will not come tomorrow, but it will come."

"Ken, Melekhi," said Tzakhi. The atmosphere in the room had suddenly shifted.

"I am assigning you as Avidan's lieutenant at Tamar," said Melekh Shlomo. "You will serve for a year at Har Megiddo learning horsemanship, chariot, and cavalry tactics. Keep the Egyptian mare my commander mentioned as your first mount. You will visit my fortresses in the north to learn the capabilities of the military and to set your sandals on the earth throughout Eretz Yisrael. It will link you with the Northern tribes. You should see the flowers in spring on Mount Arbel. With my royal robes and all their colors, I am not arrayed like even one of them. They don't labor like my servants, and they don't spin like my weavers, yet they are glorious. After your apprenticeship, Tzakhi, you will return to the Arava. You know the languages of those who pass through, you know the desert, and you know the people, especially those who might cooperate with the Edomites. Sometimes the Midianites are friends, sometimes not. You understand the Bedouin tent-dwellers, and you will be able to sense trouble. And you know the rarest beauty of the desert crocus blooming only in winter."

"Yes, Melekhi," said Tzakhi again. It was easy to see the melekh's poetic side.

Melekh Shlomo looked upward, inclining his ear as though hearing something. One of the idle scribes quickly adjusted a parchment on his lap-desk and dipped his quill into a juglet of ink. The melekh began to sing melodiously:

In that day there will not be light, cold, or frost.
It will be a unique day which is known to the HaShem;
Not day, not night;
At evening there will be light.
In that day living waters will flow from Yerushalayim;
Half of them toward the eastern sea
Half toward the western sea;
In summer and in winter will it be.
HaShem will be King over all the earth.
In that day HaShem will be one, and His Name one.
All the land will be like the Arava,
From Geva to Rimmon south of Yerushalayim
She will be lifted up, and will dwell in her place,
From Binyamin's gate to the place of the first gate,

To the corner gate, and from the tower of Hananel to the
king's wine-presses.
Men will dwell there, and there will be no more curse
Yerushalayim will dwell safely.[48]

The melekh sang the song through three times, then a small group of men whom Tzakhi hadn't noticed until now took up the words to the accompaniment of a flute player and three harpists. Together they sang and played, following the melekh through the happy tune. Once they had sung it through three times, the one who seemed to be the leader nodded to the melekh. Melekh Shlomo fell silent, letting the beautiful notes echo in the memory of the court.

Eventually, he returned his gaze to Tzakhi. He said, "Any other request, Tzakhi ben Nachshon? You simply gave me another gift. Is there nothing you want for yourself? 'A hearing heart,' maybe?"

There was a collective chuckle in the court. This is what it was said Melekh Shlomo requested of HaShem when he was crowned melekh over Israel.

"A question, Melekhi?" Tzakhi asked.

"Ahhh...a wise son," said Melekh Shlomo. "Who seeks more white in his aged hair. Ask your question."

The court responded with louder laughter.

Tzakhi wasn't sure if he was being made fun of, but he didn't care. He was used to hair jokes. "Har Karkom. Is it the Mountain of HaShem?"

The melekh smiled. "There is a reason no one knows exactly where Moshe is buried or where the Mountain of HaShem is. They

---

48   Zechariah 14:6-11

would become cultic shrines. People would worship demonic deities there. Isn't this true already?"

"Yes, Melekhi," said Tzakhi. "I saw all the altars and matzebot. But we saw things on that mountain. They did not seem ordinary."

Melekh Shlomo said, "I'm sure you did. It is a spiritual opening. When our father Ya'akov slept at Beit El, he awoke and realized he was at 'Ha-Makom,' The Place of our Temple Mount, Mount Moriah where his father Yitzchak was offered. We know Beit El is quite a distance from Yerushalayim, right?"

"Yes, Melekhi."

"The spiritual realm of Yerushalayim was stretched to Beit El. In that sense, it was Ha-Makom, the Temple Mount. The same occurred at Mount Chorev with Moshe and the Israelites. The spiritual realm of the Temple Mount was picked up and dropped over Chorev like a blanket. What the people experienced, they experienced as if they were worshiping here. Spiritual realms are movable, unlike the earth upon which we walk. When mortal men encounter the Presence of HaShem or His messengers, what are they told to do?"

"Take off their sandals," replied Tzakhi. "And they fall on their faces."

"It is because the realm of the Holy Temple has been moved to that location. Like the priests and Levites minister barefoot on the Temple Mount, so a mortal must remove his sandals to reverence the strength of that Spirit. One falls on his face as we do when we worship in the Holy Temple," said Melekh Shlomo. "Once the message is delivered, then the place reverts to its natural state. As with the cloud that led the Israelites in the wilderness, which was both fire and watery cloud, the Presence can move, stop, and linger, creating a holy space until the purpose is accomplished. Now that the Presence dwells in the Holy Temple, it remains there. It can still move, though, and create a holy space in another place. All the earth is HaShem's."

Tzakhi nodded.

The melekh continued, "So the actual mountain of Chorev is not important. It could be any mountain. The Presence of HaShem encounters human beings, yet He does not dwell in any place but His House. He may *be* in other places, for He created them all, but He *dwells* here in Yerushalayim."

"I understand, Melekhi," said Tzakhi.

"You do?"

"I do."

Melekh Shlomo chuckled, which created an echoing murmur of amusement in the chamber. "That's not something I hear often," the melekh said. "Please explain it to my court."

It felt like he was sitting in front of the scribe again. Was it better to sound foolish in front of a Torah scribe and a Temple crowd, or in front of the melekh and his court? The melekh tilted his head, raised his eyebrows, and fluttered his hand, a silent prompt.

"The mountain was not different from any other place in the Arava until the cloud formed. When the cloud disappeared, so did the Presence," said Tzakhi. "It was barely there afterward. Like when a caravan leaves Tamar. Well, maybe more than that. More like when a heavily-perfumed woman leaves a room, but the scent lingers."

"Wise hair, wise boy," said Melekh Shlomo. "Wise man, now, I hear. Mazal tov on your first visit to the Temple and Yerushalayim. Few have first entered so triumphantly, not even my abba. It is a blessing from Heaven."

"Thank you, Melekhi," said Tzakhi.

"So now our business, my wise young man. Understand the importance of Tamar. When the people of Yisrael are obedient and faithful to our covenant with HaShem, then we control that border. The boundary was set at Tamar in the time of Yehoshua. When we...depart..."

Melekh Shlomo faltered a little, his words fading, a thought interfering with the completion of his instructions. He rubbed the gold threads of his sash between his thumb and forefinger for several seconds. With a slight scowl, he continued, this time tracing the ivory etching of his throne, "When our reverence for HaShem wavers, the Edomites prevail. You must be like Captain Avidan, Tzakhi. Your attention to security must include moral security. Do not allow idols on that border. You've learned from The Levite, yes?"

Tzakhi answered, "Yes, Melekhi."

"Learn as much as you can from The Levite. I sent him there, too. He was quite a man before..."

There Melekh Shlomo stopped. He looked off, maybe seeing a memory. After a few moments, he smiled grimly. "So is it true you speak with wolves?"

"Not exactly, Melekhi. I understand them, that's all. I think they understand me." Tzakhi thought, *If you're the one who speaks the language of animals, maybe you should ask the wolves.*

The melekh stared intently at Tzakhi, jolting Tzakhi a little. *I just did.*

Was this Tzakhi's own thought?

"We will speak of this again," said Melekh Shlomo, interrupting the internal conversation. "Nu, for now, let us seal our agreement. Do you accept the commission into my army?"

Tzakhi looked at Abba, who nodded. Although they'd bowed before the melekh when they approached the Lion-Throne, Tzakhi covered his heart with his right hand and bowed again.

Melekh Shlomo's steward approached Tzakhi. He held an expensive neck ornament, an official collar of the Melekh. Tzakhi had seen one only twice when B'nayahu, commander of the army, visited Tamar. It was also given to those who did a great act of heroism in defending the melekh personally. It was a warrior collar with a royal shield pendant.

Even as Tzakhi bent his head to accept the honored ornament over Shira's concealed copper scroll, he realized he would have no more freedom than Shira. He'd escaped the fires, yet the cost was to serve the melekh. Another human soul. A better position, yes, than the conscripted Hittites, once fierce warriors who conquered as far as Egypt itself. Now the noble warriors were carrying burdens like Melekh Shlomo's donkeys. So Tzakhi would now carry the melekh's burden of protecting the kingdom.

Even so, his heart rejoiced. The Arava was home. *Whatever else would I want?*

So long ago, so long ago.
The wolf and the lamb lay down together
Across the holy mountain
The man of the earth, the woman of the sea did track.
And their child so pale with hair so black
Grew a lock of silver to find the way back.
So it will be, so it will be.

Author Notes

This is a work of fiction, so it does not rise to the academic standards of history, archaeology, Biblical criticism, rabbinic literature, linguistics, or even metallurgy. Having spent time at Tamar digging with archaeologists, sitting with a coffee on top of the fortress, hiking to Ein Tzin in the shadow of Ma'ale Akkrabim, and climbing Givat Chatzeva, I simply listened for ancient voices to tell me what their daily lives were like. What did the soldiers of Tamar watch on television on Wednesday nights?

Some things don't change. The sand is the same sand, the rocks are the same rocks, the mountains are the same mountains, the springs are the same springs, and the sun is the same sun. The gazelles, scorpions, jackals, chukars, lizards, porcupines, and wolves inhabiting the area are descendants of the ancient ones. So are the peoples.

The challenge was to consolidate all of the clues and records of the new Iron Age into the current age and into my first language, English. I beg the reader to grant the creative license needed to preserve some of the ancient language, yet to use a modern Hebrew name, such as Har Karkom or Borot Lotz.

The anachronisms were sometimes necessary to enhance readability. Are the Biblical "sons of Nevaiot" the Nabateans who later emerged as the master traders of the Spice Route? Some of the details are creative guesses. And as with archaeology and Biblical critics, the only sure thing is disagreement by the scholars. No fewer than *three* locations may have been named Kadesh-Barnea, including one at the Egyptian and Israeli border and one in present day Jordan. Permit me also the whim of the king being inspired by words only later uttered by the Prophets.

Likewise, the story of Rome's rise at the beginning of Israel's demise is based in rabbinic literature, which frowns upon King Solomon's marriage to Pharaoh's daughter. This intermarriage with an idolator is seen as the catalyst driving a reed in the uninhabitable swamp that later grew into the Roman Empire.

Scorpion's Ascent takes liberty with the literature, imagining the trajectory as growing from an ancient oracle through the rise of the later Edom, which the rabbis identified as the Roman Empire: "Blast the beast of the reed[s], the herd of bulls among the peoples, the calves.' 'Blast the beast'-that is the beast that Esav [Edom] grabbed a hold of...'The reed'-We have learned that on the day that King Shlomo married the daughter of Pharoah, Gavriel appeared and planted a reed in the Great Sea, and the city of Rome was built upon it..." (*Zohar*, Pinchas 106:740)

Roman coins are still often found at Tamar, and the author once stepped on a snake near the ruins of the Roman baths! No harm done. The moral of that story is if you decide to hike across the desert after dark to get ice cream from the Yellow station on the Eilat highway, then wear thick pants in addition to hiking boots.

If the idea of "homing donkeys" seems far-fetched, I took the idea from ancient lore. During a period of history where Christian monks lived atop a high mountain enclave, a donkey was trained to climb the path each day with provisions and return to the outpost below. Even when there was nothing to carry up the mountain on the sabbath, it is said the donkey would make the trip anyway.

The Tamar fortress is a *tel*, a multi-layered settlement. Visitors to the archaeological park will find a diagram on its top level showing the development of the fortress over the span of empires from the Bronze Age until the British occupation. It is a hidden jewel of the Arava, and it has been generously maintained by a non-profit called Blossoming Rose, including funding for the archaeological digs. Volunteers from all over the world come to clean, repair, and beautify the grounds during work weeks. As in the ancient times of the Tamar spring's caravansary, it is still a crossroads of the peoples.

Tamar goes by different names. Tamar refers to the ancient spring and district. You can see the ancient well and more recent camel troughs today (although they are dry). The mountain furnace adjacent to it is Givat Chatzeva, which means "height of the quarry." In the Hebrew Bible it is Ovot, one of the stations where the Israelites camped in the wilderness at the time of the Exodus.

Har Karkom is an arduous 4x4 journey southwest of Tamar, and as with many Biblically significant sites, is a disputed suggestion as the location of Mount Sinai. The author makes no claim to academic qualifications concerning it as the "real" Mount Sinai, but because it is located central to most of the Israelites' camping during the Exodus, its geographical location worked very well for Tzakhi's story. The reader is free not to email links to favorite videos on the subject of the "real" Mount Sinai.

If you haven't included Tamar and the Arava on your next visit to Israel, consider stopping to explore the fortress, climb the givah, or just sit on a rock and listen. Maybe the voices will speak to you. You might see a fleeting shadow on the side of a wadi.

The veil is indeed very thin there.

About the Author

Dr. **Hollisa Alewine** began her career teaching high school students for seven years before becoming a federal law enforcement officer. She earned her Bachelor of Science and first master's degree in Secondary Education from Texas A&M-Texarkana. While she continued her career with the Federal Bureau of Prisons, she completed a second master's degree in Religious Education and another in Theology in Rabbinic Studies, as well as a doctorate from Omega Graduate School. Her research has contributed to the field of correctional education.

Dr. Alewine is now retired, but continues as a programmer at Hebraic Roots Network, and she travels to teach at conferences and other venues. She is the author of *Standing with Israel,* and her Creation Gospel workbook series is an ongoing project. The proceeds of her workbook ministry support the LaMalah Children's Centre, an orphanage in Kenya, and she assists orphanages in Rwanda and India as well.

She has a book imprint called BEKY Books, (Books Encouraging the Kingdom of Yeshua), but plans to continue writing historical fiction. It has long been her desire to generate passion in young people for the land, history, archaeology, plants, and animals of the Bible. The author has spent much time in the Arava on archaeological digs, hiking, researching its geoarchaeology, and leading tours. She is a student and teacher of the Word of God.

For additional maps, archaeological updates, free downloadable educator's resource guide, author information, and information on Tamar, visit www.scorpionsascent.com.

A free ebook edition is available with the purchase of this book.

To claim your free ebook edition:

1. Visit MorganJamesBOGO.com
2. Sign your name CLEARLY in the space
3. Complete the form and submit a photo of the entire copyright page
4. You or your friend can download the ebook to your preferred device

A **FREE** ebook edition is available for you or a friend with the purchase of this print book.

_____

CLEARLY SIGN YOUR NAME ABOVE

Instructions to claim your free ebook edition:
1. Visit MorganJamesBOGO.com
2. Sign your name CLEARLY in the space above
3. Complete the form and submit a photo of this entire page
4. You or your friend can download the ebook to your preferred device

Print & Digital Together Forever.

Snap a photo

Free ebook

Read anywhere

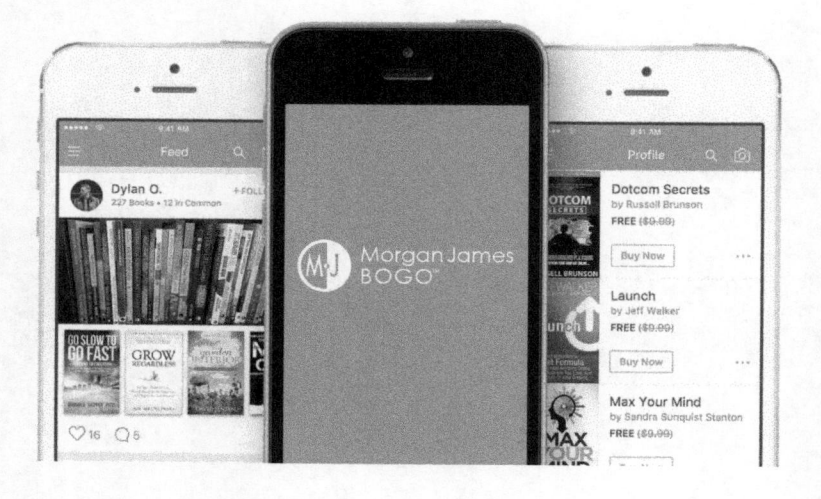